Puffin Books

Bad Boys

Even good boys (which means, I'm sure, almost everyone who reads this book) enjoy hearing about bad ones, but when I started to investigate I found that although there were lots of stories about naughty girls or bad children generally, there were very few dealing with those interesting creatures who are supposed to be made of slugs and snails and puppy-dogs' tails. So I invited some of our best-loved authors to fill the gap and this is the result.

NOTE TO PARENTS: Just as in real life the mischievous boy is often the one with too much energy and imagination, so these stories about bad boys have added liveliness and humour. It was difficult to find stories with the right degree of naughtiness. I avoided purely destructive behaviour and looked for the element of fantasy which made for variety and fun and which was not likely to be emulated by the children listening.

All the authors represented here know children and are not sentimental about them; they are aware that children are a mixture of many qualities, both admirable and disconcertingly amoral. Harassed parents will have sympathy with the characters in these stories and perhaps regard their own mischievous sons with added tolerance.

In one respect all children are alike – they love a story. It is hoped that these brief stories by practised authors will give pleasure to bad boys everywhere.

EILEEN COLWELL

Other collections by Eileen Colwell

TELL ME A STORY
TELL ME ANOTHER STORY
TIME FOR A STORY
MORE STORIES TO TELL

Bad Boys

COMPILED BY EILEEN COLWELL

Stories about boys for reading to
four- to seven-year-olds, written by

H. E. Todd
Janet McNeill
Lance Salway
Alex Hamilton
Charlotte Hough
Eileen Colwell
Gelett Burgess

Richard Armstrong
Helen Cresswell
Barbara Softly
Carolyn Haywood
Dorothy Clewes
Ursula Moray Williams
Ian Serraillier

PUFFIN BOOKS

Puffin Books, Penguin Books Ltd, Harmondsworth, Middlesex, England
Viking Penguin Inc., 40 West 23rd Street, New York, New York 10010, U.S.A.
Penguin Books Australia Ltd, Ringwood, Victoria, Australia
Penguin Books Canada Limited, 2801 John Street, Markham, Ontario, Canada L3R 1B4
Penguin Books (N.Z.) Ltd, 182–190 Wairau Road, Auckland 10, New Zealand

First published 1972
Reprinted 1972, 1973, 1975, 1976, 1978, 1979 (twice),
1981 (twice), 1983 (twice), 1985, 1986

Printed and bound in Great Britain by
Richard Clay (The Chaucer Press) Ltd, Bungay, Suffolk
Set in Monotype Baskerville

Contents

Timothy Puddle   H. E. Todd   7

Johnny Went to Church One Day   Traditional   16

The Gigantic Badness   Janet McNeill   17

The Boy Who Wasn't Bad Enough
    Lance Salway   31

The Wind That Wanted Its Own Way
    Alex Hamilton   41

Table Manners   Gelett Burgess   58

The Tidying Up of Thomas   Charlotte Hough   59

'A greedy young guzzler of York'   70

The Boy Who Made Faces   Eileen Colwell   71

'A grubby young schoolboy of Kent'   82

Timmo in the Forest   Richard Armstrong   83

'An untidy young fellow of Fleet'   94

The Wigglish Tooth   Helen Cresswell   95

Paul and the Hungry Tomatoes   Barbara Softly   107

Eddie and the Goat   Carolyn Haywood   117

Finding's Keeping   Dorothy Clewes   133

A Picnic with the Aunts   Ursula Moray Williams   149

'The Cruel Naughty Boy'   167

Andrew's Bedtime Story   Ian Serraillier   169

Acknowledgements   171

Timothy Puddle

H. E. TODD

Illustrated by Hans Helweg

Timothy Trumper likes playing with puddles. For one thing they are wet, which makes a change from all the dry things he usually plays with. For another, they splash, which is fun, and for a third, when he looks into them he can see pictures, which is magic.

The best thing about puddle pictures is that they

are always different. Sometimes they are pictures of the sky. Sometimes they are pictures of buildings leaning sideways. Sometimes, when it is fine, they are clear pictures. Sometimes, when it is raining, they are wobbly pictures.

But the most magic puddle picture that Timothy Trumper ever saw was one of a boy. It was after a heavy storm, in a puddle outside his own back door. The puddle was quite big, so he leant over it to see how deep it was, and there, looking up at him, was a boy. A cheerful-looking boy he was, too, with a wide face and a nose like a button. Timothy thought he had seen him before somewhere, but he wasn't sure where. He smiled and the boy smiled back.

'Hallo,' said Timothy.

'Hallo,' said the boy.

'What's your name?' asked Timothy.

'Timothy,' said the boy.

'That's funny,' said Timothy. 'My name's Timothy too.'

'Timothy Too?' said the boy. 'That's a funny name.'

'Not Timothy Too, silly,' said Timothy, 'Timothy Trumper.'

'Timothy Trumper's nearly as funny as Timothy Too,' said the boy, which rather annoyed Timothy Trumper, who is proud of his name.

'What's *your* name, anyway?' he asked.

'Timothy Puddle,' said the boy.

'Now who's talking about funny names,' said Timothy. 'Timothy Puddle is funnier than Timothy Too and Timothy Trumper put together.'

'All right,' said the boy. 'Then it's agreed that we both have funny names. Let's shake hands on it.'

So Timothy Trumper leaned down to the puddle to shake hands with the boy. And he made his hand all wet.

At that moment his mother called him indoors, and when she saw him shaking his wet hand she asked, 'How did you make your hand so wet, Timothy?'

'I shook hands with a boy with wet hands,' explained Timothy.

'What a silly thing to do,' said his mother, and left it at that.

On the following day there was another fall of rain, and when Timothy went outside he saw an even larger puddle by the back door. He leant over to look into it and there was Timothy Puddle staring straight back at him.

'Hallo,' said Timothy, 'so you're here again.'

'Yes,' said the boy, 'we had such fun yesterday that I thought I would come back.'

'What shall we do today?' asked Timothy.

'Well, yesterday, we shook hands,' said the boy, 'so today we'll find another way to greet each other. I know, let's rub noses like the Eskimos do.'

'All right,' said Timothy.

So he knelt down by the puddle and leant right over to rub noses with the boy. And he made his nose all wet.

At that moment his mother called him indoors, and when she saw his nose dripping she said, 'Timothy, have you got a cold?'

'No,' replied Timothy.

'Then why is your nose all wet?' asked his mother.

'A boy asked me to rub noses with him,' explained Timothy, 'and he had a wet nose.'

'What a silly thing to do,' said his mother, and left it at that.

That afternoon was wet and it wasn't fine enough for Timothy to go out again until the next day. Outside the back door there was a larger puddle than ever. Timothy looked into it and, sure enough, there was Timothy Puddle, who didn't even wait to say hallo.

'Let's play the kicking game,' he suggested.

'What's the kicking game?' asked Timothy Trumper.

'You see if you can kick my foot with your foot,'
said the boy, 'and I bet you can't.'

'I bet I can,' said Timothy Trumper.

So he stood by the edge of the puddle and then
suddenly lunged at the boy's foot with his own.
But he overbalanced and his feet went *plonk* in
the puddle, and he not only made his feet wet but
his shoes and socks as well.

At that moment his mother called him indoors,

and when she saw him hopping inside, she cried, 'Why, Timothy, your shoes and socks are sopping wet. Whatever have you been doing?'

'I've been trying to kick a boy with wet feet,' explained Timothy, if you can call that an explanation.

'Then it serves you right,' said his mother. 'Boys shouldn't kick each other.'

'But the other boy asked me to try and kick him,' protested Timothy.

'Then he must be a very silly boy,' said his mother, and left it at that.

By the following day Timothy Trumper was delighted to see that the puddle outside the back door was not only the biggest it had ever been but muddy as well. When he looked into it, he saw that Timothy Puddle was just as delighted as he was himself, but today his face was rather dirty.

'Have you got any bright ideas today?' asked Timothy Trumper.

'Certainly I have,' said Timothy Puddle. 'This puddle is just the right size for the jumping game.'

'What's the jumping game?' asked Timothy Trumper.

'You go back a few yards, then you run as fast as you can and jump *plonk* in the middle of the puddle,' said Timothy Puddle.

'That sounds great fun,' said Timothy Trumper. 'But isn't it dangerous for your face?'

'Don't worry about me,' said Timothy Puddle, 'I shall get my face out of the way in good time.'

'Are you quite sure?' asked Timothy Trumper.

'Positive,' said Timothy Puddle.

'All right, I'll try it,' said Timothy Trumper.

So he walked back a few paces, turned and ran towards the puddle and jumped as high as he could. Just as he was landing in the middle, his mother opened the back door. There was an enormous *plonk*, and not only Timothy but his mother as well was splashed from head to foot with muddy water.

'Whatever are you doing?' cried his mother.

'I'm playing the jumping game,' said Timothy. 'A boy told me to do it.'

'Oh, did he!' said his mother. 'And who is this boy who keeps telling you to do such silly things?'

Timothy leaned over the remains of the puddle and pointed to the face looking up at him. 'There he is,' he said.

'You silly boy, that's your own reflection,' said his mother.

'I thought I'd seen that face before,' said Timothy. 'But he said his name was Timothy Puddle!'

'Well, he *is* a picture of Timothy in a puddle, isn't he?' said his mother. 'You've just been talking to yourself. Next time you talk to yourself, don't tell yourself to do such silly things!'

'I'll try not to,' said Timothy Trumper.

And she left it at that.

JOHNNY WENT TO CHURCH ONE DAY

Johnny went to church one day,
*   He climbed up in the steeple;*
He took his shoes and stockings off
*   And threw them at the people.*

Traditional

The Gigantic Badness

JANET McNEILL
Illustrated by Fritz Wegner

Nobody blamed the Giant for his bigness – a giant can't help being big – but the badness of the Giant was certainly his fault, everyone in the town and countryside was sure about that.

'He's bad, that Giant is,' they grumbled, shaking their heads when they found huge footprints sunk deep on newly sown fields of corn, or hedges squashed flat. 'Never a thought for anyone but himself,' they growled if the Giant sang songs late into the night when everyone else wanted to get to sleep, or when he burnt his toast and the smell hung about the air for a couple of days. 'He's a rogue for sure,' they complained, 'if it isn't one thing it's another.' And sometimes they forgot to scold their children for talking with their mouths full, or coming into the house without wiping their feet, or sitting down at the table before their hands were washed, because these were such small badnesses, compared with the enormous outsize badness of the Giant.

Tom was one of the smallest boys in the town and he certainly wasn't the best behaved. He envied the Giant, both for his size and his badness. When you are as large as a giant there are a great many extra ways of being bad and the Giant tried most of them. He lived over the hill behind the town, but sometimes he crossed the field where the saw-mill was and if the smoke was coming out of the tall chimney he leaned over and blew down it so that the men who were working in the mill coughed and spluttered. Sometimes in the early morning he reached a finger to the school house bell hanging high against the roof, and all the children, halfway through their breakfasts, gulped and gobbled and raced into school half an hour early. Once when Tom was sailing his boats in the river the Giant decided it was a good day to take a swim farther upstream, and he enjoyed it so much that he lay on his back, kicking and splashing. Water rose up round him in fountains and then poured downstream in great waves, so that Tom's boats were swamped, and those that didn't sink were tossed against the bank with their rigging tangled and the thin stick masts smashed into pieces. That was bad enough, but a week later while Tom was out on the hill flying his new kite the Giant walked by, tangling the string of the kite in his bootlaces so that the kite came down in the middle of a gorse bush, all torn and broken.

Tom picked up the bits and carried them home. 'I'll get even with that Giant, see if I don't,' he growled all the way down the hill, and the wind heard him and laughed: 'Get even with the Giant! I'd like to see you manage it! What could you do, a boy your size, a button of a boy, a pinhole person, what could you do to beat a Giant as big and as bad as that Giant is?'

'You wait and see,' Tom promised, 'just you wait! I may not be big but I know how to be bad!'

But what could he do? Perhaps the wind had been right. Tom thought about it for a week. One day when school was over he went across the hill into the valley where the Giant lived. He had never been there before. It was a bare, grey, lonely place, rocks, little grass, and one tall leafless tree at the dark entrance where the Giant made his home.

Tom decided to hide behind a rock and wait for

the Giant. The sun had gone down, the shadows were long and blue and there was a cool moon in the sky when the Giant came home. He tramped up the valley whistling a tune to himself, and the noise he made was as loud as the town's flute band when they were out on parade. When he reached the mouth of the cave the Giant kicked off his boots, one first and then the other, hung his shabby hat on the top of the tree and went into the cave for his supper and his bed.

Tom tiptoed out from behind the rock. He stared up at the Giant's hat. It was the size of a bath. Even if he did get up to the top of the tree there would be no chance of shifting it. He leaned over the edge of one of the boots. 'He wouldn't go far without these,' he decided, and he put one of the laces over his shoulder and bent his back and heaved. But it was no use, the Giant's boot was so heavy that Tom couldn't budge it even an inch.

'No use,' teased the wind, 'no use at all. What can you do, a feather-boned boy the size of you?'

But Tom had an idea. Glue was what he needed and his father was a carpenter so he knew where glue could be found. The following evening after it was dark Tom carried a pot of glue into the Giant's valley. The boots were there. Tom emptied half of the pot of glue into one boot and half into the other and went off home to his bed.

Next morning what a commotion from the other side of the hill, what a stamping and a thumping, what a roaring and a bellowing! It went on all day, so that no one in the town heard the church clock chiming or the school bell ringing, and not a single hen in any henhouse laid a single egg. It was late in the evening and the townspeople were almost distracted when they heard first one tremendous crash and then another, then a sigh like a steam engine blowing off steam, and after that silence. 'I wonder what all that was about,' they said to each other as they collected the babies and put them to bed. Tom smiled. He knew.

That night the wind whistled down his bedroom

chimney: 'Bully for you, Tom, bully for you, bully for yoo-oo-ou!' 'I told you, didn't I?' Tom said, and he put his head below the blankets and went to sleep.

For several weeks no one heard much of the giant. 'He's lying low,' they said to each other. 'He's run out of ideas,' Tom said to himself. Saturday was the day of the big cricket match, the boys from Tom's town were playing the boys from a town nearby. It was always a very important day, and specially important this year for Tom because he had been chosen to play in the team. He ached for the feeling of the bat in his hands. This would be a day for lifting the ball high into the sky. What a match this was going to be! The teams with their supporters trooped up to the cricket pitch.

But the Giant had got there first. There he was, stretched out at his ease from one side of the pitch to the other. That was how they found him, very peaceful and comfortable, his hands clasped behind his head, one foot across the other. His eyes were closed, he was fast asleep!

They shouted and they yelled and the Giant woke up but didn't move. They tried arguing. The Headmaster of the school appealed to the Giant's better feelings. 'Better feelings? Never heard of them,' the Giant said and plucked up a cricket stump to use as a tooth-pick. The boldest of the boys poked and prodded, but it was no use. How could anyone play cricket with a giant lying in the way? And to make it worse the Giant had fallen asleep again.

'Now what'll you do? Now what'll you-oo-oo-ou do-oo-oo?' whistled the wind in Tom's ears. And Tom knew exactly what to do. He passed the word around and in no time at all the fire brigade arrived with their hoses, and it wasn't long before a drenched and dripping Giant, a gasping, soaked, indignant Giant was on his feet and off up the hill with the water running down his neck and out of his ears.

So the match was played and Tom was the hero of the day, both for the runs he scored and for the way he had got the better of the Giant. 'Beautiful,' the wind said that evening, ruffling his bedroom curtains, 'beau-eau-eau-tiful!'

But the Giant caught a cold from his wetting and he wasn't the only one to suffer from it; all the next week the town was shaken by his enormous sneezes, windows rattled, doors came unlatched, ornaments fell off the mantelpieces, babies woke and cried, there was no peace at all. 'He does it out of badness, that's what it is!' people said as another tremendous sneeze rocked the tea in their teacups and made the bread and butter slide off the plates, 'just out of badness, that's all.'

At the end of a week the sneezing stopped. 'The Giant's cold is better,' they said to each other. No sound at all came from the Giant's valley. This was very odd. 'Has he gone away?' they asked, 'he's never been as quiet as this.' 'Perhaps he's sorry,' someone suggested, but nobody really believed that. And in any case they had other things to think about. The new Town Hall was finished at last, the handsome building that had been rising slowly at the head of the street was completed, all but the weathercock which was to sit on the top of the little spire on the roof. The Mayor had invited the mayors and their ladies and the important people from towns and villages many miles round to come on Saturday for a celebration. What a day it was to be – bands, flags, fine clothes, dancing in the streets. No wonder they forgot about the Giant.

But they didn't forget about him for long because two things happened. Mr Clamber the steeplejack hurt his leg and had to stay in bed, and the builders of the Town Hall reported that the crane which was to hoist the handsome gilt weathercock to its proud place on the top of the spire had broken and there was no chance of repairing it in time. What could be done?

Nobody knew who it was who first whispered

'The Giant could help!' Somebody whispered it and somebody else heard them and soon the whisper was so loud that everybody knew about it. 'The Giant might help if he was asked. Someone will have to ask him!'

Who? Who could ask the Giant? The Mayor and two of his Aldermen went over into the Giant's valley on Friday evening, looking very serious and important. 'He won't come,' Tom said, 'catch him coming! Catch him obliging anyone!'

But to the surprise of everyone the Mayor returned to say that the Giant had agreed to come that very evening. So the policeman moved the crowds to the side of the street and cleared away some of the parked cars so that the Giant could walk without his great boots knocking into them. 'Here he comes!' the onlookers said, and at last there was the Giant himself, huge and slow, and a little shy because people were very glad to see him.

He picked up the weathercock between his

finger and thumb. 'Nice bit of work here,' he said. They explained to him how it was to be bolted into its place at the top of the spire. They handed him the nuts which looked like grains of sand in his enormous palm.

'No good,' the Giant said, 'they're too small, and my fingers are too big. I couldn't work with those, not if I tried for a year I couldn't.' Then his eyes travelled over the crowd and lit on Tom. 'But this young fellow could,' he said, 'he has the right size of hands for the job.' And before he knew just what was happening Tom had the nuts thrust into one hand and a spanner placed in the other, he felt the great finger and thumb of the Giant nip him round his middle, and up he rose into the sky!

How odd it was up there, high above the roofs, with all those pink faces staring at him from under his feet and the Giant's warm hand tight round him! With his other hand the Giant had placed the golden bird in its position. 'Now young fellow!' the Giant said as he swung Tom over beside

the weathercock. In no time at all Tom's hands had put the nuts on and tightened them.

What was that curious noise coming up from the sea of pink faces? Cheering, that was what it was, they were cheering! The cheers grew louder and louder still as the Giant lowered Tom and set him on the ground again. How splendid the weathercock looked up there in the evening sky with the last of the evening sunlight brightening its feathers. What a grand day they would have tomorrow, after all. What a good-hearted fellow the Giant was, how clever Tom had been.

'Did you hear that?' teased the wind in Tom's ear, 'cheering for you! For you and the Giant!' but the cheering was so loud that Tom took no notice at all.

The Boy Who Wasn't Bad Enough

LANCE SALWAY

Illustrated by Meredith Page

A long time ago, in a far country, there lived a boy called Claud who was so bad that people both far and near had heard of his naughtiness. His mother and father loved him dearly, and so did his brothers and sisters, but even they became angry at the tricks he played on them and the mischief that he caused by his bad behaviour.

Once, when his grandmother came to stay, Claud put a big, fat frog in her bed. Once, when the teacher wasn't looking, he changed the hands on the school clock so that the children were sent home two hours early. And once, when Claud was feeling especially bad, he cut his mother's washing line so that the clean clothes fell into the mud, and he poured a bottle of ink over the head of his eldest sister, and he locked his two young brothers into a cupboard and threw the key down a well. And, as if that wasn't bad enough, he climbed to the top of the tallest tree in the garden and tied his father's best shirt to the topmost branch so that it waved in the wind like a flag.

His parents and his brothers and sisters did all they could to stop Claud's mischief and to make him a better boy. They sent him to bed without any supper, but that didn't make any difference. They wouldn't let him go to the circus when it

came to the town but that didn't make any difference. They wouldn't let him go out to play with
his friends, but that didn't make any difference
either because Claud hadn't any friends. All the
other boys and girls of the town were much too
frightened to play with him and, in any case, their
parents wouldn't let them. But Claud didn't mind.
He liked to play tricks on people and he enjoyed
being as bad as possible. And he laughed when
his parents became cross or his brothers and sisters
cried because he liked to see how angry they would
get when he was naughty.

'What *are* we to do with you?' sighed his
mother. 'We've tried everything we can think of
to stop you being so naughty. And it hasn't made
any difference at all.'

'But I enjoy being bad,' said Claud, and he
pushed his youngest sister so hard that she fell on
the floor with a thump.

Everybody in the town had heard of Claud's
naughtiness, and it wasn't long before the news

spread to the next town and the next until everyone had heard that Claud was the naughtiest boy
in the land. The king and queen had heard of
Claud's naughtiness. And even the Chief Witch,
who was the oldest and the ugliest and the most
wicked witch in the kingdom, had heard of him
too.

One day, the Chief Witch came to visit Claud's
parents. They were very frightened when they saw

her but Claud was overjoyed, especially when she told him that if he promised to be very bad indeed she would allow him to ride on her broomstick.

'I believe your son is the naughtiest boy in the whole country,' she said to Claud's father.

'He is,' he replied, sadly.

'Good!' said the Witch. 'I would like him to join my school for bad children. We are always looking for clever children to train as witches and wizards. And the naughtier they are, the better.'

Claud was very pleased when he heard of the Witch's plan and he begged his parents to allow him to go to her school.

'At least we'd have some peace,' said his mother. 'Yes, you may as well go, if it will make you happy.'

'Oh, it will, it will!' shouted Claud, and he rushed upstairs to get ready for the journey. And so, a few days later, the Chief Witch called again on her broomstick to take Claud to her school. He said good-bye to his parents and his brothers and sisters and climbed on to the broomstick behind her. He couldn't wave to his family but he smiled happily at them as he flew away on the long journey to school, clutching the broomstick with one hand and holding his suitcase with the other.

Everybody was pleased to see him go. The people of the town were pleased. Claud's brothers and sisters were pleased.

'Now we can enjoy ourselves,' they said. 'Claud won't be here to play tricks on us now.'

Even his mother and father were pleased. 'He'll be happy with the Witch,' they said. 'He can be as bad as he likes now.'

But, as time passed, they found that they all missed Claud.

'It was much more fun when he was here,' complained his brothers and sisters. 'We never knew what would happen next.'

Claud's mother and father, too, began to wish that he had never gone away. Even though he was such a bad boy they loved him dearly and wished that they had never allowed the Chief Witch to take him to her school. And the people of the town wished that Claud would come back.

'There was never a dull moment when Claud was here,' they sighed. 'Now, nothing ever happens in our town.'

As the weeks passed, Claud's family missed him more and more.

'Perhaps he'll come back to visit us,' his mother said.

But the summer ended and autumn passed and then winter came but still there was no visit from Claud.

'He'll never come back,' said his father, sadly.

And then, on a cold night in the middle of winter, they heard a faint knock on the front door.

'I wonder who that can be,' said Claud's mother, as she went to open it. 'Why, it's Claud!' she cried. And it was. He stood shivering on the doorstep, looking very thin and miserable and cold.

'We're so glad you've come back,' said his father. 'Sit down and tell us what happened and why you've come back to us.'

'I wasn't bad enough,' Claud said, and burst into tears. And then, when he had been given something to eat and had warmed himself by the fire, he told his parents about the school and about the very wicked children who were there.

'They were even naughtier than I am,' he said. 'They turned people into frogs. They turned *me* into a frog until the Witch told them to turn me back. They were much, much naughtier than me. And even though I tried very hard indeed I just couldn't be as bad as the others. And so the Witch said I was too good ever to become a wicked wizard and she sent me away.'

'Never mind,' said his parents. 'We're very pleased to see you. We've missed you.'

His brothers and sisters were overjoyed at Claud's return. They laughed when Claud filled their shoes with jam while they were asleep. And they laughed when Claud tied them all to a tree. They even laughed when he pushed them all into the goldfish pond.

'Good old Claud!' they shouted. 'We're glad you're back!' His mother laughed when she found out he had put beetles into the tea-caddy. And his father didn't seem to mind when Claud cut large holes in his newspaper.

'Claud's back and quite his old self again,' they said, and smiled at each other.

But soon Claud found that being naughty wasn't as much fun any more. 'Nobody seems to mind my tricks,' he complained, 'even the new ones I learned at the Witch's school. People laugh when I trip them up, or tie their shoelaces together, or put ants in their hair. Why can't they be as angry as they used to be?'

So, because being bad wasn't any fun any more, Claud decided to be good instead. Not *completely* good, of course. Every now and again he would throw mud at his brothers and once he even covered the cat with a mixture of shoe-polish and marmalade. But people soon forgot that he was once the naughtiest boy in the whole country. And the Chief Witch was so disappointed in Claud that she didn't call again.

The Wind That Wanted
Its Own Way

ALEX HAMILTON

Illustrated by Gunvor Edwards

Nobody likes to wake up before they are ready,
and most people are a bit cross when something
happens that stops them sleeping when really they
should sleep a bit more. That is exactly what happened one morning to Larry, who was very fond

of his bed at night time and did not like to go anywhere near it during the day. Something woke him up when he was not ready for it.

As soon as he woke up he felt cross, because he could see straight away that night-time was almost over, so it seemed silly to try to go to sleep again. But daytime hadn't arrived yet, either, so there wasn't enough light to read a book or paint a picture. Out of the window it was a bit black, a bit white, a bit blue, a bit red, a bit yellow, a bit of everything.

But there was no use in being cross with everybody – because they were all asleep. It wasn't any person that had woken him up, it was only the wind. The wind made this funny noise in the chimney that went *Whooooo-woooo-whooo-ooooooooo* and every now and again got more excited and shrill and went *weeeeeeeeeee* and that usually ended with something in the garden or the street going *clatterbangcrash*! Larry did not really mind the noise, except he did rather wish he could see what it was the wind had broken.

He thought if he went downstairs he might be able to see better how things got broken when the wind pushed them over, so he jumped out of bed and went to the door. But first of all he told all his animals to stay in bed until he told them they could get up, because he was going to go downstairs and tell the wind to make less noise. Then he tried to open the door.

That was quite hard to do. It was terrifically stuck. But when he had turned the handle he suddenly gave such a great pull that he sat down, but at least the door was open. And in the same second the wind roared down the corridor and slammed the bathroom door shut with a shivering crash. So Larry ran down the corridor, to see if the door had broken.

It hadn't though. The wood must have been very strong. Just to see if it was really strong, he opened the door and let the wind bang it shut again. The noise was even louder than the first time, but it still didn't break. He did it just once more, to be absolutely certain, and this time a little bit of paint fell off and the key dropped out of the lock. Larry was just walking down the corridor to speak to his animals when an even bigger noise sounded all over the house.

It gave Larry a fright, until he realized it was his Daddy's voice from the bedroom, shouting 'What on earth is going on out there?' Larry realized his Daddy would be cross with the wind for waking him up too, so he thought he would just run in and mention what the wind was doing everywhere, woooo-wooo-wooing down the chimney and squealing about the garden and breaking things in the road – and crashing doors shut. The door to the bedroom where his Mummy and Daddy slept went the other way, so as soon as he turned the handle it went inside, *thump* against the wall.

His Mummy and Daddy were sitting up in bed and Larry could see they must be cross with the wind.

'It's the wind,' said Larry. 'It's a bad wind and I'm very cross with it.'

But his Mummy said 'Never mind the wind. It's you that's a bad boy running about in the middle of the night and waking everybody up.'

'Yes, go back to bed and shut the door,' said his Daddy, falling back on the pillow so that the whole bed bounced up and down.

It upset Larry to be talked to like that when he hadn't done anything. His eyes filled with tears and he could hardly speak. He said 'I'm not cross with the wind any more. I'm cross with *you*!' And he turned round and went out of the bedroom. It was hard shutting the door again, and that made him even crosser, but he managed it somehow.

He had been going to tell them how the key had fallen out of the lock and that he would put it back, but now he decided he would not do that.

Instead, he picked it up and threw it down the lavatory pan. Then he held the door and said 'You are a bad wind, and I am a bad boy, so we are friends. If you like you can shut this door with a big bang.' As soon as he let go the wind did what he asked.

The noise of his Daddy shouting had woken all his animals up, and naturally they were also very cross with him for doing it. Larry shouted out to his Daddy that he was a very bad man running about in the middle of the night shouting and waking animals up and now he could stay in bed and keep his door shut. And in fact either his Daddy had gone to sleep again, or he paid attention to what Larry said, because the door certainly stayed shut. That just made Larry determined to show them what a real bad boy was like.

At that moment the wind made a specially fierce noise down the chimney and all the animals looked a bit scared. So Larry explained that it was all right really, because the wind would be their friend. Some of the animals went on looking a bit scared, sitting there in the bed all round Larry, so he told them he was a bit fed-up with that. To make them listen to him properly he punched Teddy on the nose, dropped Rubbish the woollen cat on the floor, sat on Rags the blanket, and banged the heads of the rest together.

Then he gave them all a cuddle to cheer them up. He told them they could come downstairs to meet the wind, but they must promise not to speak because the wind hated to be interrupted. None of the animals said a word, so Larry knew that was all right.

But it turned out he could not take them all down, because there wasn't room to carry them all. So he decided to take Teddy and Rubbish and Rags, who always went everywhere. Then he went downstairs – very slowly because it was still a bit dark.

When he got downstairs he could hear the wind much better. It was a very *pushy* wind. It was going

round and round the house trying to get in somewhere. All the doors and windows were shut and
the wind sounded furious at not being able to
come in. Every now and again it would dash up
the garden path and go 'flap flap rustle' on the
front door.

When it had done that several times Larry put
all the animals down and went to open the door.
As he was pulling back the bolt he called out 'I'm
sorry, wind, that nobody let you in.' But when he
opened the door he saw it was the newspaper that
had been making the flapping sound and the wind
just rushed past.

Larry bent down to pick up the newspaper, but
as soon as he did the wind snatched it out of his
fingers and threw it in pieces all over the hall. 'You
really are very bad!' Larry said to the wind. He
was rather pleased actually, because sometimes
things are not as exciting as everybody says they
are going to be, and obviously this was a wind that
would stop at nothing if given the chance.

He was just thinking about that, when the wind took the hats off the hat-stand, one after the other, and kicked them all over the place. First Daddy's garden hat, then Daddy's going-to-work hat, then Mummy's rain-hat, then his own sou'wester. Larry wasn't so pleased about that. 'That's *my* hat!' he said sharply, and he put the sou'wester on, so the wind couldn't do anything so unfriendly again. To show he did not really mind about the other hats, though, he kicked a big dent in Daddy's black work-hat.

'Wait a minute,' said Larry. 'I'm just going to put the newspaper in Daddy's study.' He opened the study door, but the wind didn't wait. It went hurtling right past Larry and spun round and round, heaving papers out of boxes and trays and corners wherever it went, and then sending them sailing around in the air. Some of the papers went right up to the ceiling and looked as if they were never going to come down. In no time at all the whole room was a terrible mess.

'Gosh, wind,' said Larry, 'my Daddy might be very cross with you, because he's a very tidy person.'

But the wind showed no sign of calming down. Larry tried again.

'I'll tell you what, wind,' he suggested. 'Listen, I think we had better just go and sit down quietly in the front room and I will see if I can find some breakfast.'

The wind made a laughing pleased noise, so Larry shut the study door and went across the hall into the kitchen. 'Would you like tea or coffee?' asked Larry politely.

The wind could not seem able to make up its mind, so Larry took down the tea-caddy and the coffee jar and unscrewed the lids to show the wind what was inside. In two seconds the wind had half emptied them both and spread a mixture of tea-leaves and coffee powder all over the kitchen. Wherever Larry looked was turning a sort of brown colour.

'You wouldn't think two little jars could cover
the whole kitchen,' he said. 'You're not only bad,
wind, you're very clever as well.' Then he showed
the wind the inside of the marmalade to see what
would happen.

But the wind didn't take any notice of the
marmalade. So Larry helped himself to a spoonful.
Then he said 'Shall I show you how to throw the
marmalade round?' The wind seemed to be
waiting and watching, so Larry took the spoon

and shot bits of marmalade round the kitchen. It didn't spread as thin as coffee and tea, but it did make interesting shapes where it landed.

The wind made a low whistling noise like people do when they are impressed. It made Larry feel funny looking at the marmalade and coffee and tea-leaves covering the kitchen and he said, 'We won't have any more breakfast now. We'll go and sit in the front room with the animals until it gets daylight properly. You can go outside again if you like.'

He said 'Good-bye' to the wind at the front door and took Teddy and Rubbish and Rags to sit on the armchair by the window in the front room. They all listened to the wind outside and after a time the noise it was making began to make Larry feel a little uncomfortable again. He thought perhaps the wind might be upset because he had not let it stay inside when it looked as if it was going to rain.

Then there was the most tremendous cracking

sound, like a bit of wood breaking. He stood up in the armchair and saw that the wind had smashed a branch of the tree where Mummy often tied her washing line. Next the twigs at the end of the branch began crackling up against the glass of the window pane.

Although the animals had promised not to speak, Larry could see that they all wanted him to let the wind back in again. He said 'All right, but this is the last room we're going to be bad in. After that the wind will just have to make up its mind to go away, because I don't want to be bad all the time.'

Then he undid the catch on the window and the wind dived through with a great howl of glee. It sucked the curtains out, twisted them round and round like a rope and fairly thrashed them against the wet walls outside. They were pink before, with a silver pattern, but soon nobody would ever have known they were pink, and the silver parts had vanished under the dirt.

The broken branch came swaying in through the opening, dropping wet slimy leaves everywhere. Worst of all, it poked a long woody finger out and nicked the heads off a whole row of Mummy's tulips. One vase was overturned and smashed, while the water flowed across the carpet. Like birds landing on a lake, all the cards on the mantelpiece suddenly went floating through the air to join the mess.

Larry jumped down and stood in the middle of the room with both arms in the air. 'I have never seen such a bad wind in all my life!' he cried.

Almost as soon as he had said it, the wind began making less noise. The rain, which had been going sideways in big heavy blobs, now turned into something very fine and soft, falling straight down. The broken branch pulled itself slowly back out of the window and hung sadly down to the ground. The curtains stopped flapping and waving and dancing, and leaned against the window frames as if they were completely tired out.

The wind made a sort of hissing sound, which got quieter and quieter. Larry thought it was saying 'See you some other Saturday,' but it was hard to tell exactly, because it was moving farther and farther away down the street.

It was getting to be real daylight. Larry was a tiny bit cold, so he collected his animals and they all got under the cushions of the armchair. Perhaps they all went to sleep for a while, because the next he knew his Mummy and Daddy were standing beside the chair speaking to him. They weren't just cross. They were very angry.

'You've torn up the newspaper!' said Mummy.

'You've ruined my hat!' said Daddy.

'It'll take hours to get the kitchen clean and nobody can have tea or coffee this morning,' said Mummy.

'I'll have to spend my whole weekend putting my bills in order again,' said Daddy.

'You've destroyed these curtains . . .'

'Soaked the carpet . . .'

55

'My flowers!' said Mummy.

'My apple tree!' said Daddy.

'I've never known anybody be such a bad boy in all my life!' they both said together.

'It was the wind,' said Larry. 'It wasn't me that was bad, it was the wind. It was a very bad wind. I've never known such a bad wind in all my life.'

'It's just as bad helping somebody else be bad, as it is being bad yourself,' said Mummy. 'And none of this would have happened if you hadn't been helping the wind to be bad.'

'And for the rest of the day you can help it be good,' said Daddy.

Actually, Larry did quite like helping people be good as well as bad, and in the end he was friends again with everybody. But he did think it was a bit of a cheek for the wind to just go away like that, and let him take all the blame when it was only partly his fault.

That night when they went to bed he said to all his animals, 'Next time the wind wakes us up we'll just go to sleep again, and he can go and be bad in somebody else's house.'

TABLE MANNERS

The Goops they lick their fingers,
And the Goops they lick their knives;
They spill their broth on the table-cloth;
Oh, they live untidy lives.
The Goops they talk while eating,
And loud and fast they chew,
So that is why I am glad that I
Am not a Goop. Are you?

Gelett Burgess

The Tidying Up
of Thomas

CHARLOTTE HOUGH

Illustrated by the author

Thomas was a rough, untidy child. His kind uncles
and aunts had given him a Noah's Ark and a farm
and a zoo and soldiers and cars and games and
paints and books and goldfish and a rocking-horse
and a blackboard and a Red Indian costume and –
oh, everything you have ever wanted.

But he was so *rough*, and so *untidy*!

His poor mother was distracted. She didn't know what to do about Thomas.

One day he fetched the scissors out of her work-box and pulled all the stuffing out of poor old Teddy. Teddy would have had to be thrown away if Thomas's mother hadn't collected it and sewn him up again.

'You're a very naughty, wasteful, silly little boy!' she scolded him, 'And you don't deserve all those lovely toys.'

Another day Thomas was playing in the kitchen while his mother was writing letters, and when she went in to make tea she found he had mixed up the sugar and the flour and the barley and the tea and he had broken the coffee-pot and spilt the vinegar.

'Oh Thomas, Thomas!' she cried, 'I only hope you're ashamed of yourself!'

But Thomas wasn't ashamed of himself, not in the least bit! He thought he was really very clever.

He put the blackboard chalks in the pencil

sharpener and made coloured powder and used it for gunpowder to make indoor fireworks with, but that didn't go off right, so he left all the firework things in a heap on the floor and scribbled on the faces of the people in his books to make them into black people. He took the tyres off the cars and mixed them all up with the cowboys and Indians, and, oh so many naughty things you would hardly believe it.

Of course somebody as naughty as Thomas never goes to bed without making a terrible fuss and to-do about it. First he would refuse to go at all, and after his bath he always had to be sent back to the bathroom because he hadn't washed his ears, and then back again because he hadn't cleaned his teeth. He had always either broken his comb or torn his pyjamas. By the time he was really and truly in bed and asleep his parents felt absolutely exhausted.

'We shall really have to do something about that boy,' said Thomas's father.

'Oh yes, I quite agree, we shall really *have* to,' said his mother, 'but what? We've tried everything.'

When everyone was in bed, the toys woke up and cautiously felt their bruises and sorted themselves out. What a rustling and whispering there was! The farmer was collecting up the flock of sheep from amongst the bricks, while Mr Noah and the zoo-keeper tried to track down *their* animals, and a toy soldier climbed stiffly out of the goldfish-bowl, shaking the water out of his busby. A squeaky trumpeting came from under the book-case where the little zoo elephant had got pinned down under a battered police-car. Luckily his friend the woolly elephant was able to pull him free and help him back to the broken cardboard box which was shared by the zoo with various paper-clips, lumps of plasticine, and other odds and ends.

'We shall really have to do something about that boy,' said the kangaroo, as she searched for her baby amongst the dressing-up clothes (she eventually found him in the paint-box).

'Oh yes, I quite agree, we shall really *have* to,' said the woolly snake, 'but what? I can't do much to help. I've completely lost one eye and my head's getting all loose because he always picks me up by it though I distinctly heard them telling him not to.'

'You're lucky,' said a tin bus bitterly. 'Do you know, he used me instead of a hammer the other day? I've got some nasty sharp edges and hardly any paint left and I used to be such a beautiful red.'

'Well, look at me,' put in the rocking-horse. 'It's shocking, it really is. No mane, no tail, no stirrups, no nothing and all my bolts worn and bent. Wobbling-horse would be a better name after all my rough treatment.'

'We're getting dangerous,' said the toys. Everybody knew what happened to dangerous toys and there was a thoughtful silence, broken only by a sneeze every now and then as the poor toys breathed in the dust. Thomas's room was impossible to clean properly; it was always too messy.

'Well,' said the rocking-horse at last, raising his head, 'I don't like to be unkind but we really can't go on like this. There is nothing else for it. We shall have to take a firm line.'

In the middle of the night Thomas woke up. Something was scratching him. 'Bother!' he said, 'I must have left something in my bed!' And he ferreted about and found a small tin turkey. 'That's funny!' he said, 'I don't remember playing with that up here!' And he threw it out and closed his eyes.

But Thomas couldn't go to sleep. However much he rolled over in bed he always managed to lie on something hard and spiky. In the end he got up, switched the light on, and pulled his bed to pieces. There amongst his bedclothes lay all the farm animals with their sharp little legs. There were pigs in the pillowcase, sheep in the sheets, cows in the coverlet, bulls in the blankets and hens and ducks and milking girls *everywhere*. Thomas shook them angrily out on to the floor and then he tried to make his bed again.

Thomas wasn't good at making beds. He had an uncomfortable night.

At half past seven he was up and dressed, without anybody even calling him once, pleased to leave that horrid, cold, lumpy heap of bedclothes. There was such a lot of extra time that he started to get his things ready for school.

Before long he went running into the kitchen to find his mother. 'Look at my nature book!' he cried indignantly, holding it up before her eyes.

'Well, it's a nasty messy-looking thing,' agreed his mother, 'but so are all your other books.'

'But this is a *school* book!' cried Thomas. 'You can't scribble on *school* books – you'd get into awful trouble. Nobody ever does. We aren't allowed to!'

His mother looked at it more closely. 'But you

have done, dear,' she said mildly. 'With all your coloured chalks.'

'But it wasn't me that did it!' shouted Thomas, nearly in tears.

'Now Thomas,' said his mother, putting down the milk-jug and turning to face him, 'I know you're a rough, untidy boy but at least you always used to be a truthful one. I didn't scribble on your book and neither did your father. That only leaves one person who could have, doesn't it? Now sit down and eat your breakfast and don't let me ever hear you tell a lie again!'

Thomas opened his mouth, and then he looked at his mother's face, which was unusually firm, so he changed his mind and shut it again. Silently he ate his breakfast and silently he went upstairs to the bathroom to clean his teeth.

Silently he gazed at the row of empty toothpaste tubes. Silently he fetched a bowl and a cloth and silently he cleaned the toothpaste off the bath, the floor, the walls, the door. Somebody had been enjoying themselves! He worked hard. His father would soon be coming in to shave.

Ten minutes later, Thomas rushed madly into

the hall to get ready for school and a moment later another loud wail reached his mother's ears. 'I can't wear *this*!'

'What's the matter now, dear?'

'There aren't any buttons on my coat!'

'Nonsense dear, they can't all have gone, not all at once!'

'They have! Just look!'

'Good gracious! So they have!' said his mother in astonishment. 'Whatever made you do such a thing? You've cut them all off! Well, there's no time to sew them on again now. You'll just have to go as you are. Really, Thomas, I can't think what's the matter with you! I'll just have to hide all the scissors in the house. Every single pair. You don't seem to have any *sense*!'

'But listen!' cried Thomas desperately. 'I . . . didn't . . . do . . . it!'

'Thomas! Remember what I said,' warned his mother. 'Untidiness is one thing. Telling lies is another.'

'But don't you see? THE TOYS DID IT!'

'Well, dear, if the toys did it I can't say I blame them, seeing the way you treat them. Perhaps now you'll realize what it's like, being treated that way. Perhaps it will teach you a lesson!'

And do you know, it did!

'How extra specially clean and tidy you are, Thomas dear,' people say admiringly when they come to tea, and they wish *their* little boy or girl was as good!

Some people even say the toys have extra special expressions on their faces, but that seems to be going a bit far, really, don't you think?

A greedy young guzzler of York,
Filled his tummy with ice-cream and pork,
  With cream cakes a score,
  And chocolates galore,
Said his brother, '*You* waddle, *not walk!*'

E. C.

The Boy Who Made Faces

EILEEN COLWELL

Illustrated by Gunvor Edwards

There was once a boy called Fred. He was not at all a nice little boy. He left his toys out in the rain, he hated washing, he pulled the cat's tail, he drew on the wallpaper, he said 'Shan't' when anyone asked him to do things.

One day he found out that he could make such

ugly faces that it upset everyone who saw them. Soon he gave up his other tricks and just made faces instead. Only to look at him gave little girls bad dreams and when his friends played with him and were winning he would make such horrible faces that they were put off and lost the games. 'It's not fair!' they said and they wouldn't play with him any more. When Fred's favourite aunt came to see him he pulled such a frightful face that she never came back again but just sent a card on his birthday.

The only person who didn't see him making faces was his mother – he didn't want to upset *her*. So she was surprised when visitors screamed or fainted because of the horrible faces Fred was making behind her back. 'Freddie is such a kind little boy,' she said, 'and he always has a nice smile.'

Fred wouldn't listen to his friends and relations when they warned him that his face would stay that horrid shape if the wind changed. 'Pooh!'

said Fred rudely and stood out in the wind when it was changing to see what happened. But nothing did.

His father spanked him but that only made him twist his face more because the spanking hurt. At school he spent a lot of time in the corner looking at the wall so that the teacher shouldn't see the faces he was making. She said it made her forget what she was supposed to be teaching – not that the children minded that.

It didn't matter what people said or did, Fred made faces and that was that.

One day Fred's Uncle Charles came to see him. He had been in far-away foreign countries for years and years and this was his first visit since Fred was born. Fred was very excited about his uncle's visit for he would bring a present of course – all proper aunts and uncles do – and he might know some different kind of faces Fred could make, the kind they made in Peru or Timbuktu.

Uncle Charles did bring a present, a carved

wooden monkey, which Fred thought was rather dull. Uncle Charles looked quite ordinary anyway, except that he carried a walking stick everywhere and sometimes pointed it at people who annoyed him. When he did so the stick lighted up at the end with a blue crackly light and the people stopped whatever they were saying and went away very quickly. Otherwise nobody worried for they thought it was probably the odd way people be-haved in the foreign countries where Uncle Charles had been living.

Sometimes, too, Uncle Charles would put his hand in his pocket and bring out some strange creature, a jerboa or a salamander perhaps. 'Oh well,' said Fred's mother, 'Charles was always interested in Nature.' Perhaps so, but Fred won-dered why the salamanders and other creatures were all colours of the rainbow and why they suddenly vanished. Sometimes Fred would ask his uncle why he carried these strange creatures in his pockets and where they went to when they disappeared. 'Strange creatures in my pockets? Rubbish, boy!' said Uncle Charles. 'You can see for yourself there are none there,' and he turned his pockets inside out.

At first Fred didn't make faces at Uncle Charles because he was too interested to see what his uncle would do next and, besides, he was a little nervous of him. But one day he forgot and made a frightful face. Uncle Charles watched him with interest. 'Not bad,' he said kindly. 'Do it again.' Fred did. 'Hmm . . .' said Uncle Charles thoughtfully. 'Would you like to enter for a competition in making faces? You might do well.'

'Oh, could I?' asked Fred, delighted. 'Where is the competition?'

'There's a fair in the town,' said Uncle Charles. 'There should be one there. Let's go, boy.'

So off they went together, Uncle Charles carrying his walking stick as usual. 'How nice to see Freddie and his uncle such good friends,' said Fred's mother.

At the fair there were all sorts of things to see – a Fat Woman, performing dogs, a very large man who could lift heavy weights marked ONE TON. There were hot-dog stalls and candy-floss stalls and several kinds of roundabouts. Fred chose to ride on one which had cars and aeroplanes, but Uncle Charles preferred a jungle roundabout and rode on a lion, his long legs dangling on either side. Fred *thought* he heard the lion roar and saw it shake its mane when Uncles Charles got on its back, but he must have been mistaken, of course.

Several times when they had to pay for seeing things or riding on things, Uncle Charles put his hand in his pocket and brought out one of the strange creatures. Fred had to remind his uncle that they wouldn't do instead of money. 'Dear me, where can those have come from?' said Uncle Charles as the salamanders and jerboas disappeared. The people at the fair watched in astonishment.

Fred wasn't very good at throwing the wooden

balls at the coconut shy, but however badly he threw, he was surprised to find that he nearly always hit the coconuts. Then he noticed that when Uncle Charles pointed his stick at the balls, they turned round in the air and hit the coconuts with a bang. Fred collected a whole armful of them and the man in charge didn't like it at all. 'Clear off, guv'nor,' he said crossly. 'It ain't fair!'

So Uncle Charles gave him all the coconuts back except one for Fred to take home.

Then they came to a large tent which had a poster outside – COMPETITIONS. TRY YOUR LUCK. Fred and his uncle paid their money and went in. In a dark corner sat an old man with a rubbery kind of face. He was saying in a tired, hoarse voice, 'Make faces and win a bicycle!' over and over again.

'Ha! Now's your chance, boy,' said Uncle Charles.

Fred went up to the old man and so did three other children. 'Wot you does,' said the old man, 'is to stand on this 'ere platform and make as many different horrid faces as you can, see. The one that makes the most faces and keeps it up longest wins the bicycle.'

The first boy was so nervous that, instead of making horrid faces, he looked quite pleasant and gave up almost at once. The next entrant, a girl, did so well that the old man told her to wait. The third to enter was Fred.

'Now, Fred, do your best. Don't let me down,' said Uncle Charles.

Fred began. He made face after face while Uncle Charles looked on approvingly.

Fred went on, changing expressions as fast as he could. At first he enjoyed it, but soon his face began to get tired. 'Isn't that enough?' he asked, but the old man didn't answer but only stared at him with his mouth open like a fish.

'Keep it up, boy,' said Uncle Charles, clapping loudly.

Now Fred was making such horrible faces and

so fast that he even frightened himself when he caught sight of his face in the mirror on the canvas walls.

'Can't I stop now?' he asked imploringly.

'Don't you want to win?' said his uncle. 'Come, come, get on with it.'

On and on went Fred until his face ached all over. 'Do let me stop!' he begged.

'Faster, *faster*, FASTER!' said his uncle relentlessly – and Fred burst into tears. 'I can't bear it any longer,' he sobbed.

'STOP!' exclaimed Uncle Charles and he pointed his stick at Fred and the old man. A blue light crackled and Fred found himself at his uncle's side. His face had stopped moving and it felt stiff all over.

'Next!' said the old man hoarsely.

'I want to go home,' said Fred, sniffing.

'But you might win the prize! The other boy may not do as well as you did.'

'I don't care what he does,' said Fred. 'Let's go home, *please*.'

'Better luck next time,' said Uncle Charles. 'You'll improve with practice.'

'I don't want to practise. I don't want to make faces ever again,' said Fred.

Next morning Uncle Charles had gone before Fred woke up. Fred still felt he didn't want to make faces. He went to school and the teacher didn't put him in the corner once and the other boys seemed quite friendly, although Fred couldn't think why they had changed.

One morning Fred looked in the mirror and saw a boy he didn't recognize, a boy with a cheerful expression and a nice, friendly smile. It was himself! And behind him he thought he saw his Uncle Charles, and his uncle was smiling too. The next moment there was no one there. How could there be?

A few days after, a large packing case arrived addressed to Fred. Inside was a marvellous bicycle with all the extra gadgets Fred had longed for. The carved wooden monkey Uncle Charles had given him made a splendid mascot for the handlebars.

'Now, whoever could have sent this to you, darling?' asked his mother. Fred was sure it was Uncle Charles but he never said so to anyone for, after all, Uncle Charles was in a faraway country and couldn't possibly know that Fred had stopped making faces.

Or could he, perhaps?

A grubby young schoolboy of Kent,
Didn't know what the word 'washing' meant,
He bathed in his vest
And neglected the rest,
That dirty young schoolboy of Kent.

E. C.

Timmo in the Forest

RICHARD ARMSTRONG

Illustrated by Beryl Sanders

Timmo lived halfway up a very steep hill and
Scruffy was the boy next door. Their houses were
exactly the same; but the gardens were different.
Scruffy's garden was all neat and tidy with little
flower-beds here and there and lots of vegetables.
Timmo's garden was wild. It had grass growing in
it shoulder-high and big clumps of brambles.

83

There were also some old apple and pear trees, just right for climbing. So they always played in Timmo's garden and that is where the forest comes in.

The forest was big; so big even boys old enough to ride bicycles with two wheels had been lost there; and both Timmo and Scruffy had been told to keep out of it.

It started – the forest, that is – just on the far side of the hawthorn hedge and it completely covered the rest of the hill. In fact you could see no end to it. It just went on and on for ever, right up into the sky. There were roads through it, of course; but every one of them was closed with an iron gate and on every gate was a big notice-board. *Private. Trespassers will be prosecuted,* said the notice-boards and both Timmo and Scruffy knew this meant *keep out*. They had been told so more times than they could remember.

Nobody knew how many trees there were in the forest but Timmo and Scruffy often wondered.

'I bet there's a hundred. There must be!' said Scruffy one day.

'More like a thousand; maybe a million!' was Timmo's guess. And forgetting all about the notice-boards, they crawled through a hole in the bottom of the hedge, hoping to find out who was right.

Now the queer thing about that forest was that the trees all grew in straight rows. It didn't matter which way you looked, there they stood in long straight lines. Like lines of soldiers on parade they were, marching criss-cross and sideways as well as up and down all over the hillside. This made them very difficult to count because when you stopped to take a breath, there was nothing to show you how far you had got and you had to start all over again. And besides, there were too many of them anyway; more than two small boys could ever count in a month of Sundays. So presently Timmo and Scruffy gave up counting. But they still went on climbing up the hill.

It was a bit spooky in there under all those trees. The sun was shining brightly outside but it couldn't reach through the tops of the trees because they were so close together. So although it wasn't exactly dark, it wasn't light either; and everything was greeny-coloured and very still. It was also very quiet and Scruffy could hear his own heart beating.

'Thump, thump, thumpity, thump!' it said, and suddenly he remembered the notice-boards.

'You know we shouldn't be here,' he said. 'Let's go back.'

'You do what you like,' said Timmo. 'But me, I'm going right to the top.'

'But we'll get into trouble,' said Scruffy.

'Nobody will know; not if you don't tell them,' answered Timmo and pushed on.

Scruffy followed; but the farther they went and the tighter the forest closed in around them, the louder Scruffy's heart thumped and the less he liked it. He knew they ought not to be there.

'Suppose,' he said, panting at Timmo's heels, 'Just suppose we got lost?'

'Nobody ever gets lost going up a hill,' snorted Timmo, scornfully. 'Not if he doesn't want to, that is.'

'Why not?' asked Scruffy.

That was another difficult question; but not for Timmo. He had already worked out the answer, so it seemed very simple to him. They were going up and when the time came to go back home, they would just turn round and walk down again.

This shut Scruffy up for about two minutes. Then he started looking over his shoulder and worrying about what might be lurking in the shadows under the trees.

'Suppose there's a lion in there or a tiger!' he said.

'Don't be silly!' said Timmo and then, very patiently, he explained that such animals don't live in England. There are badgers and foxes, red deer and wild ponies, rabbits and stoats and a whole lot of other things; but not lions, and not tigers either.

'Except in the zoo,' said Scruffy.

'Well, yes,' agreed Timmo. 'Except in the zoo, of course.'

'All right, then!' Scruffy looked over his shoulder and went on supposing. 'Suppose a lion in the zoo escaped; suppose he came here to hide; suppose he saw us and suppose he jumped right out on top of us!'

Timmo thought Scruffy didn't know much about lions and told him so. 'They never jump out on people, only when they are hungry,' he said.

'This one is very hungry,' said Scruffy. 'I mean if he has run away from the zoo, he won't have had anything to eat for a long time, so he's bound to be hungry, isn't he?'

Timmo had to agree the lion, if there was one, would be hungry but that made no difference to him. Not really. He was going to the top of the hill and if a lion or tiger jumped out at him on the way, he would just climb up a tree and wait till it was gone.

They walked on and now in spite of his brave words, Timmo was looking over his shoulder as often as Scruffy. He wasn't afraid, of course; not Timmo; but he wasn't taking any chances either. So he kept a very good look-out as they went. He was also very quiet and if he spoke at all, it was in a whisper. Perhaps they had been told to keep out of the wood because of what they might meet there?

In the end, they were both so busy staring into the shadows and looking out for things like lions they forgot to watch the path they were following. This really wasn't very clever of them because when they did look at the path again, it wasn't going up any more. It wasn't going down either, but straight on along the top of the hill.

'You know something!' said Scruffy. 'We're lost.'

'We can't be!' said Timmo. 'I told you, we've only got to go down the hill again and we'll come back to the hawthorn hedge.'

'I know all that,' agreed Scruffy, 'but which way is down?'

Then Timmo saw that the hill, still covered with trees to the very edge of the sky, went downwards on *both* sides of the path; and it looked as if Scruffy was right for once; but Timmo wouldn't say so. Not yet.

'This way!' he said, diving off the path into the trees to the right, just as if he knew the way.

Scruffy followed.

On they went down the hill; and on and on for a long time. They saw all sorts of exciting things. There was a stag with wide-spreading antlers; a fox with bright, beady eyes and a bushy tail, slinking through the undergrowth, and a herd of wild ponies. Some of the ponies were black, some brown and their hooves made a noise like thunder a long way off. One of them had a foal running beside it. The foal was white; it had very long legs and its mane and tail streamed out as it ran. They also saw lots and lots of funny-looking toadstools under the trees; but no hawthorn hedge with houses on the other side of it.

And presently Timmo noticed that the hillside had stopped going down again. It was going up instead; but it was still covered with trees and they all stood in lines whichever way you looked – up and down, criss-cross and sideways – and every tree in sight was the same as the one standing next to it.

Now Timmo knew for sure that Scruffy was right and they were lost in the forest and he wished he hadn't made Scruffy come into the forest with him; but he didn't say so and went on pretending.

On and on they wandered, up one hill and down another, then another after that; and still there was no hawthorn hedge and no end to the trees either.

So at last with his feet aching, his face and hands all scratched with brambles, his clothes torn on briers and his legs plastered with mud to the knees, even Timmo could pretend no longer. They were well and truly lost in the forest. He was just opening his mouth to say so when he heard the sound of a motor car, quite close.

'This way!' he shouted instead, diving into the

trees again. But this time he really knew what he was after. It was the motor-car; and running as fast as he could, he led Scruffy towards it.

They ran and ran, shouting as loudly as they could; and suddenly they burst out of the trees into a wide road. It wasn't hard and tarry like the one running past the houses where they lived, but soft and covered with short grass and tufts of heather. And there right in the middle of it was a Land-Rover with a man in it. He was the forest ranger. It was his job to look after the trees and he was very cross with Timmo and Scruffy for being there. He gave them a real wigging and made them promise never to go into the forest again.

But at last he forgave them and he said he would drive them back home himself before they got into any more mischief. They were just in time for tea.

Timmo would never admit that he had been lost that day; but he kept his promise and so did Scruffy.

An untidy young fellow of Fleet,
Preferred both his shoes on wrong feet,
His laces untied,
His mac torn inside,
And his shirt hanging out at the seat.

E. C.

The Wigglish Tooth

HELEN CRESSWELL

Illustrated by Shirley Hughes

This is the story of Jon (short for Jonathan) and Alison, the girl who came to live next door.

The day she moved in Jon had been out playing and came home hungry. All the way up the road he could smell other people's dinners being cooked, and in the end, he *ran* home.

'The new people have moved in next door,' cried his mother as he came in.

'Is dinner ready?' asked Jon. 'What is it? Sausages?'

He peered past his mother's elbow to the steaming plates. It *was* sausages. Fat, brown, juicy sausages – and what was his mother saying? He sat at the table and waited, sniffing.

'. . . and perhaps we could ask if she'd like to come to tea?' came his mother's voice.

'Ask who?' he demanded. He hadn't even eaten his dinner yet, and she was already talking about tea. Not that he minded.

'What *is* for tea, anyway?' he asked.

'You're not listening to a word I'm saying,' said his mother. She plonked his dinner in front of him. After that, he certainly wasn't listening.

'What's for pudding?' asked Jon when his plate was empty.

'An apple.'

'*That's* not a pudding!' said Jon. 'Why can't

we have a proper pudding? Why can't we have jam roly-poly?'

'Apples are good for you. And they're good for your teeth. Are you going to have one or not?'

'I'll *have* one,' he said. 'But it's still not a proper pudding.'

He picked a large green apple, streaked with red, and bit hugely into it.

'I s'pose I can always have two,' he said through his first mouthful. 'Or three. Or four.'

His mother was washing up, and did not answer.

Suddenly he had an odd feeling that something was wrong – at least, not exactly wrong, but *different*. Something in his mouth. He swallowed a few morsels of apple and put a finger gingerly into his mouth. Gently he pushed it against his bottom teeth, and with a little shock, felt something move. It was a tooth!

He poked his tongue forward and pressed it hard – but not too hard – against the back of the tooth. It moved again. In fact, it *wobbled*.

Jon tested it from the front again with his finger. It was a queer feeling – a bit frightening and a bit exciting. It was frightening because the tooth was *him*, it was part of him, and if it came out, part of him would have gone. But it was exciting as well, because it meant he was soon going to be grown-up. First teeth were 'baby' teeth, everybody said. When they came out, they made room for *real* teeth, grown-up teeth, *big* teeth.

'All the better for eating with,' thought Jon, and picked up the apple again. He bit very carefully this time, but he felt the tooth move and was scared because it had all happened so quickly, so he put the apple down again.

'I don't think I'll bother with this apple,' he said, after a minute.

'O *Jon*! I do wish you wouldn't start things if you're not going to finish them. What a waste!'

Jon said nothing. He nearly told his mother about the wigglish tooth, and then didn't. It was a secret, hidden inside his own mouth. Nobody else knew about it. He pressed his tongue against it again, to make sure the tooth was still loose. It was. *Very* loose.

'There's that little girl, out in the garden!' cried his mother. 'Go out and make friends, Jon, and see if she'd like to come to tea!'

Jon went out into the garden to see what the girl was like. She looked up and saw him.

'Hello!' she said. 'My name's Alison. What's yours?'

'Jon,' said Jon. 'Short for Jonathan.' He stared at her. She was older than him – about seven, he decided. She came right up to the fence and stared back.

'How old are you?' she asked.

'Five and a half and nearly six.'

'I'm seven and a quarter,' she said.

'I've got a friend who's nearly eight,' said Jon. It was nearly true. It was a cousin, really, not a friend. The girl gave a little laugh and Jon saw the gaps in her teeth. She had two teeth missing on the top row.

'I've got a wigglish tooth,' he said then, before he could stop himself. 'It's going to come out, I can feel it.'

This time when she laughed he took a closer look and saw that there were one and a half teeth missing, not two.

'That's nothing,' she said then. 'I've lost dozens of teeth. Dozens and dozens.'

Jon looked at her, wondering how many dozen teeth she had altogether and what a dozen was, anyway?

'Haven't *any* of yours come out, then?' she went on.

'One's *going* to,' said Jon. 'I can feel it with my tongue. It's all wigglish.'

Alison laughed again, and there again were those two maddening grown-up gaps in her teeth.

'What are you laughing at?' Jon asked.

'At you! It's such a funny word. Wigglish!'

'It *is* wigglish,' said Jon.

'O it's not a *bad* word,' she said. 'Just funny.

Lucky you. I wish *I'd* got a loose tooth. I could do with ten pence.'

'What do you mean?'

'Don't you know? When a tooth comes out, you put salt on it and put it under the edge of the carpet and next morning it's gone, and there's a ten-penny piece there instead.'

Jon watched her. Was she teasing him?

'Honest?' he said at last. That was a whole week's pocket money.

'Honest. Ask your mother, if you don't believe me. Look what I've got.'

She bent and picked something up from the grass. It was a bow and arrow. She drew back the string, took aim, and let the arrow fly. It went right across the garden in a long, beautiful curve.

In that moment Jon forgot his wigglish tooth. Suddenly, more than anything in the world, more even than a gap in his teeth, he wanted a bow and arrow.

'Can I have a go?' he cried. 'I can get through the fence. There's a hole down there.'

'It's new,' said Alison. 'I only had it this morning. You're too small for a bow and arrow. You might break it.'

'I wouldn't!'

'You might. Look,' she added, a little more kindly, 'why don't you ask *your* mother for one? They've got them at that little shop on the corner. Only forty pence.'

Jon turned his back on her and raced to the house. He could see his mother through the kitchen window, still busy at the sink.

'You'd better get your money box out,' she said, when he had finished talking. So he did. It was a post box with a small door that opened with a special key. He shook it. It did not feel very heavy.

'Thirty-two pence,' said his mother when they had emptied out the coins. 'You'll have to save some more. You'll be able to buy one on Saturday, when you get your pocket money.'

'But it's only Monday today!' cried Jon.

'It's not very long to wait. You can't have everything you want just like that. You must learn how to save.'

Jon went out again. He didn't go right down the garden this time, because although he wasn't actually crying, he nearly was. He stood watching Alison letting fly her arrows and chasing after them.

'I hate her!' Jon thought. 'Show off, with her great teeth and bow and arrow!'

His tongue reached for the comforting feel of his wigglish tooth. It seemed even looser than it had the last time he'd felt it.

'I only *need* another ten pence,' he thought. 'That's all. Mean thing!'

Backwards and forwards went Alison's arrow, backwards and forwards went the wigglish tooth as Jon's tongue pressed and squeezed against it.

Then the answer came.

Ten pence! Ten pence a tooth, that was what she'd said. Jon didn't even stop to think. Back he went into the house.

'Can I have an apple, please?' he asked.

'An *apple*? You've only just left half a one.'

'Can I have that half, then, please? If you just cut the brown bit off, it'll be all right.'

'*I* don't know,' she sighed. 'Here you are, then. Aren't you going to make friends with that little girl?'

'I have,' said Jon. 'I don't like her.'

He went straight out again and took a very deep breath and bit hard into the apple. He felt nothing. It was just like any bite into any apple. He started to chew, and all at once there seemed to be a funny taste in his mouth – not an *apple* taste at all. And then he felt something small and hard against his tongue and put up his hand to take it out and there was the tooth!

It lay on his hand very small and white – smaller by far than it had *felt* when it was in his mouth – and certainly not looking worth ten pence – and his tongue flew to the gap that was left and waggled to and fro in it, and the gap felt *enormous*, absolutely enormous.

'Mum!' yelled Jon. '*Mummy*! My tooth's come out! My tooth's come out!'

It was the most marvellous thing that had ever happened to him. He'd got a gap, a real, grown-up gap in his teeth, and it hadn't even hurt!

'But why didn't you tell me it was loose?' cried

his mother, when she had hugged him and admired the tooth and his brand new gap.

'It wasn't exactly loose,' said Jon. 'Just wigglish.'

'Well! You are grown up now,' said his mother. 'And you'll have to leave that tooth under the carpet tonight, and see what you find there in the morning.'

Jon grinned. He knew very well what he would find. He went out again into the garden. He wanted to show Alison his brand new gap. And tomorrow, there would be a bow and arrow. He'd probably get his mother to make him a black patch to wear over one eye, like a pirate. All the best pirates had gaps in their mouth.

He bared his teeth in an enormous smile, and went to meet Alison . . .

Paul and the Hungry Tomatoes

BARBARA SOFTLY

Illustrated by Diana John

It was summertime. Paul had taken Stumpers on
holiday with him for three weeks. As a matter of
fact Stumpers went everywhere with Paul. He was
an elephant and Paul had had him for as long as
he could remember.

For the first week of their holiday Paul and Stumpers stayed by themselves with Paul's uncle, Danny. For the second and third weeks, Paul's mother and father came down to join them in Danny's house.

Danny lived alone, except for Mrs Bunce from the near-by town, who came in to cook and clean for him, a shaggy dog called Solomon, two white doves called Dum and Dee, and two hedgehogs called Piggen and Wiggen, who came every night for their saucers of milk. Danny was very glad to have the hedgehogs because they ate up all the slugs that tried to eat his lettuces.

'This evening,' said Paul, when he and Stumpers were in the garden after tea, 'we could ask Danny if he will let us put out the saucers of bread and milk for the hedgehogs and wait up until they come for their supper.'

Stumpers' long trunk curled with excitement.

'Stay up late after dark?' he said. 'I've never seen the hedgehogs eating their supper, but I've heard them rattling their saucers when they think it's feeding time.'

At that moment Danny came into the garden.

'Talking about feeding time and feeding the hedgehogs,' he said, 'reminds me that I've forgotten to feed the tomatoes. They will have to wait until tomorrow now, because I must finish writing some letters and then we'll go out and catch the last post. Would you like to water the lettuces and beans, Paul, while you are waiting for me?'

Danny hurried into the dining-room. Paul and Stumpers walked up the twisty path through the apple orchard to the garden shed at the foot of the red brick wall. In the shed were the garden tools, the lawn-mower and wheelbarrow, the boxes for seeds and pots for plants and the watering-cans. High up on the shelf were bottles and jars which Paul and Stumpers had been told not to touch.

'You water the beans and I'll water the lettuces,' said Stumpers, as they picked up the cans and raced back to the tap outside the kitchen door. Up the path they went again to the vegetable garden, Stumpers to the row of fat little lettuces, Paul to the tall runner beans which were already climbing their poles and showing their scarlet flowers.

Against the brick wall in the sunniest part of the garden were the tomato plants which Danny had forgotten to feed.

Stumpers set down his watering-can, pushed his trunk in the top and sucked up as much water as he could to shower over the thirsty lettuces. When the watering-can was empty and Stumpers' trunk only gurgled in the bottom, Stumpers stood still and looked at the tomatoes. The plants were dark green and leafy and they had small clusters of yellow flowers on their stems. Stumpers huffed and thought.

'What are you doing?' asked Paul.

'Thinking,' said Stumpers, 'about tomatoes.'

'If I had to wait until tomorrow before I had anything to eat, I should be very hungry,' said Paul.

'So should I,' said Stumpers.

'I think Danny is so busy that we might feed the tomatoes for him, don't you?' said Paul.

'Huff,' breathed Stumpers. 'But what do they eat?'

Paul didn't know.

'Bread and milk like the hedgehogs, peas like the doves, biscuits and bones, like Solomon?' asked Stumpers.

Paul shook his head. 'They haven't any teeth, so they couldn't munch up peas or biscuits or bones. If we made up a mix – a kind of soft mix – eggs and milk and breakfast cornflakes –'

'We could pour it round them and give them something to eat. Honk!' snorted Stumpers happily down his trunk. 'How many are there?'

'Ten,' said Paul, counting carefully. 'We'll need the big mixing-bowl for the food and a watering-can for the milk.'

'Danny will be pleased,' said Stumpers, as they ran back to the kitchen. 'Shall we tell him?'

'No,' said Paul. 'We'll give him a surprise.'

They found a mixing-bowl and a wooden spoon in the kitchen cupboard.

'I'll stir,' said Paul. 'Your trunk is so long you can reach all the shelves. I'll stir and you bring everything out here.'

He sat on the step and waited while Stumpers rattled about in the larder and at last came out, his arms full of packets and cartons, his trunk carefully wrapped round three milk bottles.

'Six eggs, breakfast cornflakes, a packet of sugar and a brown loaf,' said Stumpers.

'We'll give the crust to the birds,' said Paul, holding the spoon in both hands to mix everything together and gripping the bowl between his knees so that it would not slide about.

'Anything else?' he asked. 'It's very sticky.'

There were more rattlings as Stumpers hunted in the larder.

'Salad cream,' he called. 'A bottle of vinegar and some orange juice.'

Paul thought the orange juice would be best and it was slowly stirred into the mixture making it a soft, creamy yellow.

'Yellow mix,' said Stumpers, tasting it with his trunk. 'Honk!'

Then they took the tops off the three milk bottles and poured the milk into the watering-can. It was heavy and as Stumpers walked up the garden path behind Paul, the milk slopped out of the spout and made little splashes of white along the path.

The mixing-bowl was heavy, too. When Paul reached the row of tomatoes, he had to put the bowl on the ground and ladle out spoonfuls of yellow mix for each plant. Soon he had made a thick yellow circle round each stem; there were dollops of mix on most of the leaves, dollops on the flowers, dollops trickling everywhere, and a lot of dollops all over Paul. Stumpers followed behind, happily honking to himself, swinging his trunk in time to his honks, showering every tomato plant with milk.

'It's not a watering-can any longer, it's a milking-can,' he said.

Then –

'Paul! Stumpers! What on earth are you two doing?'

It was Danny, carrying his letters in his hand and running up the garden as fast as he could. He did not look at all pleased.

'We thought we would feed the tomatoes to-night as a surprise for you, because we didn't want them to be hungry,' said Paul, wiping his yellow-mix hands down his shorts.

Danny looked at the row of tomatoes; he looked at the yellow mixing-bowl, at the milking-watering-can, at Paul and Stumpers.

'You know who is going to be hungry now, don't you?' he said. 'You are, because the shops are shut and there is no bread for your supper, no milk to drink, no cornflakes or eggs for breakfast, no sugar, no orange juice. *This* is what tomatoes are fed on.'

He took down one of the sticky, black bottles from the shelf in the garden shed.

'This – mixed with water.'

'Oh,' said Paul.

'Ah,' said Stumpers.

That night Paul and Stumpers went to bed early. They did not stay up to feed the hedgehogs, although Danny had found enough milk left in a milk-jug to give Piggen and Wiggen bread crusts and milk for their supper. Paul and Stumpers did not really have any supper. There were only biscuits and as many glasses of water as they wanted.

Stumpers curled his trunk under his arm as he settled on the end of Paul's bed.

'Feeding time for hedgehogs and feeding time for tomatoes, but no feeding time for us,' he said.

'I'm glad we didn't take the doves' peas or Solomon's dog biscuits,' said Paul. 'The sooner we go to sleep the sooner we shall be able to go out shopping and buy our breakfast.'

'Honk!' snorted Stumpers. 'But it's a long time to wait.'

And it was.

Eddie and the Goat

CAROLYN HAYWOOD
Illustrated by Richard Kennedy

Eddie was the youngest of the four Wilson boys.
There was Rudy, aged twelve, the twins, Joe and
Frank, who were nine, and Eddie. Eddie was
seven.

Eddie was very fond of animals. He often
brought stray animals home with him. Stray cats,
stray dogs, birds that had fallen out of their nests,

snails, snakes; anything that was alive, Eddie loved.

For the past week the children in Eddie's class had been having the fun of owning a baby goat. A farmer who was a friend of Miss Weber, their teacher, had given the baby goat to her and she had brought it to school. The children had been reading the story of Heidi and they were all interested in Heidi's goat. Of course the children wanted the little goat to stay at school forever, but Miss Weber said she would have to take it back to the farmer, because there really was no place to keep a goat.

'Couldn't we keep it where we have it now?' George asked. 'At the back of the school on the grass?'

'Couldn't we build a house for it?' asked Eddie.

'No,' said Miss Weber, 'we can't keep the goat here. But the farmer said that if anyone would like to have the goat and would take proper care of it, he'd be glad to give it away.'

Eddie could hardly believe his ears. 'You mean for nothing?' he cried.

'That's what the farmer told me,' said Miss Weber.

'Well, I could have it,' said Eddie. 'I could keep it at my house. I could take care of it.'

'Are you sure, Eddie?' Miss Weber asked. 'Are you sure your father and mother wouldn't object to your having a goat?'

'Oh, sure!' said Eddie. 'My father and mother love goats. They'd be delighted to have a little goat.'

'I think you had better ask them first,' said Miss Weber.

'I don't have to ask them,' said Eddie. 'I can take the goat.'

'Ask them first,' said Miss Weber.

At dinner that night Eddie said, 'Papa, you know the baby goat I told you about?'

Mr Wilson said, 'What about the baby goat, Eddie?'

'Well, it's an awful nice little goat,' said Eddie. 'I could have a very enjoyable time with that little goat.'

'A goat!' exclaimed Mr Wilson. 'That's just what we need! A goat! Probably the only way we can ever get rid of the junk in the basement – get a goat to eat it!' And at this point Mr Wilson got up to go to a meeting. 'Yes, indeed!' he said. 'A goat is just what we need!'

The following day when Eddie went to school he said, 'Miss Weber, I can have the goat. My father said it was just what we need.'

'Very well, Eddie, the goat is yours,' said Miss Weber. 'Take it away this afternoon.'

'I brought a dog collar and a lead,' said Eddie. 'Do you think she'll go with me?'

Miss Weber thought the goat would go with Eddie and it did. And a whole crowd of children went too. But Eddie had a hard time walking with the goat, because the goat was always walking sideways instead of forward. This made the going very slow and the children were always bumping into each other because the goat bumped into them. One by one they left Eddie until he and the goat were alone.

The closer Eddie got to his home the more he thought of his father, and the more he thought of his father the more he felt that he was not going to like the little goat. There was something about the way Father had said, 'A goat is just what we need,' that made Eddie feel perhaps he would not be pleased.

Eddie decided to sit down on the kerb and think the matter over. The goat lay down beside him. Here Mr Kilpatrick the policeman found them as he was driving home in his police car.

Mr Kilpatrick stopped and said, 'What are you doing with that goat, Eddie?'

'I was taking her home but now I don't know. I am afraid perhaps my father won't like it.' Then Eddie told Mr Kilpatrick how he had happened to get the goat.

'Did you ask your father whether you could bring the goat home?' Mr Kilpatrick asked.

'Well, not exactly,' said Eddie. 'I told him we had a goat at school and he said, "That's just what we need, a goat!"'

'He did?' said Mr Kilpatrick, raising his eyebrows. 'That doesn't sound too good to me.'

'You don't think he'll like the goat, Mr Kilpatrick?' said Eddie, looking up at the big policeman.

Mr Kilpatrick shook his head. 'I have me doubts,' he said, 'very grave doubts.'

Eddie sat with his chin resting in the palm of his hand. The little goat nuzzled its nose under Eddie's arm. Eddie patted it on the head. 'I think if my father knew this little goat, he would like her,' he said.

'Maybe!' said Mr Kilpatrick. 'But you made a big mistake in not talking to him about it first. You should have told him all the nice things about the goat and got him interested. You should have smoothed the way. That's what you call diplomacy. If you take this goat home now, your father will probably throw it out.'

'Out where?' asked Eddie, with a startled face.

Mr Kilpatrick waved his arms around. 'Oh, he'll probably telephone for the R.S.P.C.A.'

'What's that?' Eddie asked.

'The Royal Society for the Prevention of Cruelty to Animals,' said Mr Kilpatrick.

'But I'm not going to be cruel to my goat,' said Eddie.

'Nevertheless,' said Mr Kilpatrick, 'that's where it will go. You should have used diplomacy.'

Eddie sat deep in thought. The goat was taking a nap. Mr Kilpatrick sat in his car, looking down at the two on the kerb.

In a few minutes Eddie looked up. His face was brighter. 'Mr Kilpatrick,' he said, 'couldn't you keep my goat until I can use what you said on my father? I don't want my goat to go to the Cruelty to Animals.'

'Oh, Mrs Kilpatrick wouldn't like it,' said Mr Kilpatrick. 'She wouldn't like it at all.'

'But it would only be until tomorrow. I could talk to Papa tonight,' said Eddie.

Mr Kilpatrick thought for a few minutes. Then he said, 'Well, come on. We'll take it along. We'll see whether Mrs Kilpatrick will have it overnight.'

Eddie got up and this woke the goat. He lifted it in his arms and put it on the front seat, between Mr Kilpatrick and himself. In a moment they were off. They turned a few corners and the car stopped in front of Mr Kilpatrick's white fence.

Mrs Kilpatrick was cutting flowers in her garden. She looked up when the car stopped and waved her hand. She watched Mr Kilpatrick step out of the car and she watched Eddie step out. When she saw the goat, she said, 'Now what in the name of peace are you bringing home?'

'It's just for the night, Katie,' said Mr Kilpatrick. 'I'm helping my friend Eddie here.'

'It's my goat, Mrs Kilpatrick,' said Eddie. 'And

Mr Kilpatrick says I have to talk to Papa, so he won't give it to the Cruelty to Animals. Mr Kilpatrick says I have to use – what kind of dip is it, Mr Kilpatrick?'

'Diplomacy,' said Mr Kilpatrick.

'Well!' said Mrs Kilpatrick. 'See that that goat is out of here tomorrow.'

'It's all right, Katie,' said Mr Kilpatrick. 'It's just for tonight.'

Mr Kilpatrick had a great big wooden box with a hinged lid. He turned it on its side and propped the lid open. 'This will make a good house for a goat,' he said. 'I'll go over and get some straw from the stable and you won't have to worry about your goat. She'll be comfortable for the night.'

'Thanks, Mr Kilpatrick,' said Eddie. 'Any time you want me to keep anything of yours I'll be glad to. Any turtles or anything.'

'That's O.K., Eddie,' said Mr Kilpatrick. 'Just talk to your father tonight. I'll bring the goat over tomorrow after school.'

Eddie patted his goat on the head and ran off with a light heart.

When Eddie reached home, he told his brothers about the goat. They thought it would be wonderful to have a goat. 'But I don't think Dad will let us have it,' said Rudy.

'Well, just leave it to me,' said Eddie. 'I'm going to use dip . . . Well, anyway, I'm going to use it.'

At dinner that evening Eddie said, 'Papa, you know that goat we had in school?'

'Goat?' said his father. 'Oh, yes! What about it?'

'Well, it's an awful nice goat,' said Eddie.

'They smell terrible,' said Mr Wilson.

'This one doesn't,' said Eddie.

'Eddie,' said his father, 'if you are thinking of bringing that goat here, you can forget it right now.'

'Oh, Papa!' Eddie groaned.

'I think it would be swell to have a goat,' said Frank.

'We could harness it to the wagon and it could pull the groceries home for Mother,' said Joe.

Eddie beamed on Joe. He began to think that Joe was smarter than Rudy.

'Goats give milk,' said Rudy. 'Good milk.'

Mr Wilson looked at his four sons and said, '*No goat!*'

The next day when Mr Kilpatrick's car appeared in front of the Wilsons' house, Eddie ran out. 'Here's your goat,' said Mr Kilpatrick. 'Did you fix things up with your father?'

'Oh, Mr Kilpatrick!' cried Eddie. 'I have to use some more dip . . . What kind of dip did you say it is?'

'Diplomacy!' Mr Kilpatrick shouted. 'Diplomacy!'

'Well, I have to do it some more,' said Eddie. 'Will you keep the goat tonight?'

Mr Kilpatrick did not look as though he were going to keep the goat for five more minutes until Eddie said, 'Please, Mr Kilpatrick, just tonight.'

'O.K.!' said Mr Kilpatrick, 'but you have to take her tomorrow. Mrs Kilpatrick won't stand for it. That goat ate all the flowers in the front garden and Mrs Kilpatrick won't stand for it.'

'Just tonight, Mr Kilpatrick,' said Eddie. 'Just tonight. Please.'

Mr Kilpatrick drove off with the goat and that night at dinner Eddie said, 'Papa, you know that goat we had at school?'

'Yes, Eddie,' said his father. 'What about the goat now?'

'Well, it's an awful nice goat,' said Eddie.

'So you said before,' said Mr Wilson.

'A goat would eat the grass and we wouldn't have to cut it so often,' said Joe.

Mr Wilson looked round the table. '*No goat!*' he said. 'Positively no goat!'

The following day was Saturday. After breakfast Eddie went over to Mr Kilpatrick's to see his goat. As he walked up the path from the front gate,

Mrs Kilpatrick called out, 'Eddie Wilson, you get that goat out of here! It ate up my flowers and this morning it ate up one of Mr Kilpatrick's woollen socks. You take that goat home with you.'

'Oh, Mrs Kilpatrick!' said Eddie. 'You'll have to keep it for me just one more night. I think my father likes the goat better every day and I think he will let me have it tomorrow.'

'Well, if it eats up one more thing, out it goes,' said Mrs Kilpatrick.

At lunch Eddie said, 'Papa, you know that goat?'

'Yes, Eddie,' said his father.

'Well, it's an awful nice goat,' said Eddie.

Mr Wilson looked at Eddie's mother and they both laughed. 'O.K.!' said Eddie's father. 'But let me tell you this. If it smells, out it goes.'

Eddie's face broke into a wide grin.

'Hurrah!' cried the twins.

'Swell!' shouted Rudy.

'Where is the goat?' Mr Wilson asked.

'It's over at Mr Kilpatrick's. He's keeping it for me.'

When lunch was over, Eddie and his three brothers went over to Mr Kilpatrick's to get the goat. When they arrived, Eddie was carrying a package in his hand.

Mr Kilpatrick opened the door. 'Papa says we can have the goat,' said Eddie, 'but only if it doesn't smell.'

'Well, it doesn't smell much,' said Mr Kilpatrick. 'It's only billy-goats that smell real bad.'

'I can fix that,' said Eddie, opening his package. 'I bought some scent at the store. It's gardenia.'

When the little goat saw Eddie, she ran to meet him. 'She knows me,' Eddie cried, as he rubbed gardenia scent all over the goat.

There was a great deal of excitement over getting the goat to the Wilsons' because Mr Kilpatrick offered to give Eddie the big wooden box that had been the goat's house for the past two nights. It was too big to go into the boot of Mr Kilpatrick's car and for a while it looked as though the house could not be moved.

Then Eddie had an idea. 'I know!' he said. 'Let's see if Mr Ward will bring the fire engine over.'

Mr Kilpatrick telephoned to Mr Ward, and about half an hour later Mr Wilson saw the fire engine stop in front of his house. On the front seat sat Mr Ward and Eddie with the goat between them and in the back were the other three boys with the big wooden box.

As Mr Wilson helped the boys to carry the box to the back of the garage, he said, 'Phew!'

'What's the matter?' asked Eddie, looking frightened.

'I smell gardenia,' said his father.

'Sure,' said Eddie, 'that's my goat. Nice, isn't it, Papa?'

And so they named Eddie's little goat Gardenia.

Finding's Keeping

DOROTHY CLEWES

Illustrated by Shirley Hughes

'It's a find,' Shaun said, '– and finding's keeping.'

'That's right.' Patrick pushed closer to his brother to get a better look. The black wallet looked important – and fat.

Shaun opened it. It bulged with notes – pounds and five-pounds, and with something that looked like a cheque book but wasn't.

'American Traveller's Cheques,' Shaun read out, very slowly because he had only just learned to read and they were long words – except that the first word was one he knew very well. His eldest sister had gone to live in America. At the time his mother had cried a lot because America was such a long way from Ireland, but now she was glad because Moira was doing so well and was so happy. One day they might all go and join her. But one day didn't mean this year, or next year. It could mean never. It was like the bicycle he had been wanting as long as he could remember: one day, his mother always said, and he still hadn't got one.

'It will belong to a visitor,' Patrick said. They came in the spring – like migrating birds, he'd heard his father say – looking for roots. It had given him an instant picture of a land that was bare of grass and trees and flowers, because without roots nothing could grow. He said now to Shaun: 'They must have dropped it while they were gathering roots.'

Shaun shook his head. He was two years older than Patrick, six, coming up to seven and he knew they weren't the kind of roots Patrick was thinking about. 'It's something to do with family,' he told him, '– like Moira living in America but her roots are here in Ireland.'

Patrick said: 'You mean – whoever this belonged to might have lived here, once?'

'That's right. Or their father or their grandfather.' Shaun was counting the money. 'There's enough to buy a bicycle,' he said. Not a second-hand one which he would have been delighted with, but a brand new one with high cow-horn handle-bars, and with a bell, and with side mirrors so that you could see traffic coming up from behind.

'Will it buy me a bicycle, too?' Patrick asked.

'You're too little for a proper bike,' Shaun said, 'but there'll be enough left over for a tricycle or a scooter.'

'I'll have a scooter,' Patrick said. On a bicycle

you were a long way off the ground, a scooter was so low that you could jump off any moment you liked.

'We'll have to go to Tralee,' Shaun said. Tralee was the nearest real town. In their own village of Ballymore there was only one shop which was also a Post Office. You could buy toys there as well as food and stamps, but nothing as big as a bicycle.

Shaun was putting the money back in the wallet after counting it when he saw the airline tickets. He knew at once what they were because they were just like the one Moira had had to buy so that she could fly in an aeroplane all the way to America.

'What's the matter?' Patrick asked him. Shaun was looking as if he had gone suddenly a long way away: not as far as America, but nearly.

'Tickets,' Shaun said, '– two of them.'

'What good's tickets?' Patrick asked. 'They won't buy anything.'

'Yes, they will,' Shaun said, his voice squeaky

with excitement. London/Cork/Shannon/New York, it said on the tickets – and Moira lived in New York.

'But it's miles and miles away,' Patrick reminded him.

'No, it isn't: not in an aeroplane,' Shaun said. He was remembering what his father had said to comfort his mother when it was decided that Moira should go to America: 'No distance at all,' his father had said. 'Be there for lunch and back in time for tea. When we have a windfall that's what we'll all do.' Well, he and Patrick had got the windfall and that's just what they could do.

'Shannon,' Shaun said, 'that's where the Airport is. It isn't so very far away.'

'Too far to walk,' Patrick said.

With all that money they ought to have been able to get there by bus, but buses didn't run through Ballymore. 'We'll hitch-hike,' Shaun said. Boys and girls did it all the time when they came visiting from across the sea. Sometimes big cars stopped for them, and sometimes small cars, and always sooner or later, something stopped.

Shaun stood at the side of the road and waved a hand as he had seen the boys and girls do but nothing stopped for them and after a while they both sat down on the grass by the roadside.

'If we can't get to Shannon we can't use the tickets,' Patrick said. He was thinking it would have been much simpler to go into Tralee and buy the bicycle and the scooter – and then there was the clip-clop of hooves and a voice they knew called:

'Would you be wanting a lift, at all?'

It was Mr Murphy with his donkey cart, taking his milk churns to the cooperative. The cooperative was the big factory where all the milk went to be bottled. After that it was sent round to customers in the villages and towns.

'We have to go to Shannon Airport,' Shaun said, scrambling up on to the donkey cart and pulling Patrick up beside him.

'Oh, the Airport, is it?' Mr Murphy said. 'It'll be your sister Moira coming home, I'm thinking.'

Shaun didn't want to say Yes and he didn't want to say No, so instead he said: 'She flew to America from there.'

'It's a great day when they come back home,' Mr Murphy said. He, too, had a daughter in America, but she hadn't done as well as Moira Rafferty and wouldn't be able to afford to come home for a good bit longer.

They clip-clopped down the dusty road between the hedgerows, Mr Murphy's milk churns making a cheerful clatter. The birds sang high in the sky and the cud-chewing cows lifted up their heads to see who was passing by.

'Isn't it a wonderful thing, now,' Mr Murphy said, 'that you can be getting to and from across half the world in the time it takes to drive my donkey to the factory and home again.' He shook his head. 'The world is shrinking, so it is.'

Now they were catching up with other carts

taking other milk churns, and now and again there was a little race between the donkeys to see who would get there first – and then in no time at all they were at the factory.

'I'm sorry I can't take you any farther,' Mr Murphy said, 'but there's Micky O'Connell. He comes from thereabouts. Sit tight now while I have a word with him.'

He came back almost at once. 'Aren't you the lucky ones?' he said. 'Micky will be glad to have you along.'

Micky O'Connell worked on a big farm. The farmer had so many cows that the milk they gave filled more than a dozen churns. A donkey cart would have been no use at all so he had to use the farm motor van.

'I don't go all the way to the Airport,' Micky told them, 'but it won't be any trouble for you to get a lift from where I drop you.'

After Mr Murphy's donkey cart the motor van seemed to gobble up the road, and the villages, and the towns. Micky dropped them at a cross-roads where one of the arms of a sign-post said:

SHANNON AIRPORT 6 MILES.

'A great choice of transport you'll have from here,' Micky told them, 'but mind you don't take just any or your Ma'll tan the hide off me.' He looked at his watch. 'About now Kevin O'Brien comes along on his way to the Airport. You'll know his lorry by the crates of bottles piled high. Tell him you're friends of mine.'

A lot of motor cars went whizzing by, most of them full of people and baggage; others were going too fast for their passengers to see anything but the road in front of them – and then a lorry turned the corner.

Shaun and Patrick heard the jingle of its load even before they saw it.

Shaun put out his hand. 'Are you Mr Kevin O'Brien?' he asked the young man leaning out of the cab.

'Now how would you be knowing that?' the young man asked.

Shaun explained.

'Oh – that Micky O'Connell. Sure, any friend of his is a friend of mine,' the young man said. 'The Airport's the very place I'm going to.' He got down and gave the boys a leg up into the cab which was so much higher than Mr Murphy's donkey cart and even higher than Micky O'Connell's motor van. 'Do you see what I'm carrying?' Kevin said. 'Soft drinks. Hundreds and hundreds of bottles in those crates behind, all going to the restaurant at the Airport. People get thirsty waiting for aeroplanes.'

Patrick was thirsty right now. He said: 'When we get to the Airport I'll buy one.'

'You're going plane watching,' Kevin said. 'I used to do that, still do when I get the time.'

Shaun said: 'We're not going to watch, we're going to fly – to New York.'

'Oh yes,' Kevin said. 'I used to play that game, too. Anywhere the planes went, I was on them.'

They could see the Airport ahead of them now – the terminal building, the runways, the control tower – and a plane just taking off.

'Too bad you missed that one,' Kevin said, 'but there'll be another taking off in a minute.' He stopped at the terminal building and they scrambled down. 'Happy landings,' he called to them.

The booking hall was filled with a great jostle of people. A voice called over a loud speaker: 'Passengers for New York now boarding at Gate 6 . . .'

'What's this now?' the man at the Gate said, taking the tickets Shaun held out to him.

'Two tickets to New York,' Shaun said.

'So you'll be Mr and Mrs Regan,' the man said.

A wave of laughter rippled through the crowd of passengers behind Shaun and Patrick.

'Take them along to the office,' the man said to his assistant.

'What will they do to us?' Patrick whispered to Shaun.

Shaun shook his head. He didn't dare to think.

The big man behind the desk looked at them sternly. Ever since Mr Regan had notified them of the loss of his wallet he had been waiting for it to turn up – but not quite like this. He began to quote

from the note-pad in front of him: 'Two tickets
to New York, a few traveller's cheques, and £50.'

'£52,' Shaun said, taking the wallet out of his
pocket and putting it on the desk.

'You mean – you didn't spend any of it?' the
man asked.

Patrick said: 'We were going to buy a bicycle
and a scooter –'

'. . . and then we saw the tickets and we thought
we'd go and see my sister,' Shaun finished for him.
'She lives in New York.'

'Well, what do I do with you?' the man said,
and now he was looking even more stern.

You could go to prison for stealing, Shaun was
sure of that – and he saw themselves locked up in a
dark little room with bars at the window and
nothing to eat but bread and water, perhaps for
ever, because £52 was a lot of money. He'd been
so excited at finding the air-line tickets that he
hadn't read enough of the writing on the tickets to
see that they belonged to someone.

The man was talking again, reading from the note on his pad: '... but it says here: "If the wallet is returned the finder is to be rewarded."'

Shaun could hardly believe what the man was saying, but there he was taking two of the notes out of the wallet: not one-pound notes, but five-pound notes. He held them in his hand, uncertain about handing them over – and then, deciding, put them back into the wallet.

'That's a lot of money for you two boys to be given when I'm not sure you deserve it.' There was a long silence and then the man said: 'Well, do you deserve it?' He glared at them across the desk.

Shaun opened his mouth to answer him but he couldn't make any sound come.

'I'll have your names and address,' the man said, pulling a note-pad towards him.

They didn't deserve the reward and they weren't going to get it. 'Shaun and Patrick Rafferty,' Shaun said. 'Ballymore.' There were only six families in the village, there was no need of a street name.

'Well, Shaun and Patrick Rafferty,' the man said – and now Shaun was sure it was going to be the little dark room for them and nothing but bread and water to eat – 'the wallet's been returned and the reward has to be handed over. I'll be sending it to your parents and they must decide if you deserve it.' And now Shaun thought there was the beginning of a twinkle in the man's eye. 'It won't get you to New York to see your sister,' he said, 'but it might buy a bicycle and a scooter if you're not too choosy. Second-hand was good enough for me when I was your age.'

'You mean – you aren't going to lock us up?' Shaun said.

The man shook his head. 'Not this time, but in future, remember – finding is *not* keeping.'

'I'm glad we're not going to New York,' Patrick said, as they walked from the Airport.

'Me, too,' Shaun said. 'Aeroplanes go too high

and too fast. You don't see anything.' It couldn't be anything like as good as riding high up in the cab of Kevin O'Brien's lorry, or in Micky O'Connell's farm motor van, or on Mr Murphy's donkey cart – or on a bicycle or a scooter, when they got them.

'Besides, we don't have to go looking for roots,' Patrick said, '– they're right here.'

A Picnic
with the Aunts

URSULA MORAY WILLIAMS
Illustrated by Fritz Wegner

There were once six lucky, lucky boys who were
invited by their aunts to go on a picnic expedition
to an island in the middle of a lake.

The boys' names were Freddie, Adolphus, Edward, Montague, Montmorency and little John
Henry. Their aunts were Aunt Bossy, Aunt

Millicent, Aunt Celestine, Aunt Miranda, Aunt Adelaide and Auntie Em.

The picnic was to be a great affair, since the lake was ten miles off, and they were to drive there in a wagonette pulled by two grey horses. Once arrived at the lake they were to leave the wagonette and get into a rowing-boat with all the provisions for the picnic, also umbrellas, in case it rained. The aunts were bringing cricket bats, stumps and balls for the boys to play with, and a rope for them to jump over. There was also a box of fireworks to let off at the close of the day when it was getting dark, before they all got into the boat and rowed back to the shore. The wagonette with Davy Driver would leave them at the lake in the morning and come back to fetch them in the evening, at nine o'clock.

The food for the picnic was quite out of this world, for all the aunts were excellent cooks.

There were strawberry tarts, made by Aunt Bossy, and gingerbread covered with almonds baked by Aunt Millicent. Aunt Celestine had prepared a quantity of sausage rolls, while Aunt Miranda's cheese tarts were packed in a tea cosy to keep them warm. Aunt Adelaide had cut so many sandwiches they had to be packed in a suitcase, while Auntie Em had supplied ginger pop, and apples, each one polished like a looking glass on the back of her best serge skirt.

Besides the provisions the aunts had brought their embroidery and their knitting, a book of fairy tales in case the boys were tired, a bottle of physic in case they were ill, and a cane in case they were naughty. And they had invited the boys' headmaster, Mr Hamm, to join the party, as company for themselves and to prevent their nephews from becoming too unruly.

The wagonette called for the boys at nine o'clock in the morning – all the aunts were wearing their best Sunday hats, and the boys had been forced by their mother into their best sailor suits. When Mr Headmaster Hamm had been picked up the party was complete, only he had brought his fiddle with him and the wagonette was really very over-crowded. At each hill the boys were forced to get out and walk, which they considered very unfair, for their headmaster was so fat he must have weighed far more than the six of them put together, but they arrived at the lake at last.

There was a great unpacking of aunts and provisions, a repetition of orders to Davy Driver, and a scolding of little boys, who were running excitedly towards the water's edge with knitting wool wound about their ankles.

A large rowing-boat was moored to a ring on the shore. When it was loaded with passengers and provisions it looked even more overcrowded than the wagonette had done, but Aunt Bossy seized an oar and Mr Headmaster Hamm another – Auntie Em took a third, while two boys manned each of the remaining three.

Amid much splashing and screaming the boat moved slowly away from the shore and inched its way across the lake to the distant island, the boys crashing their oars together while Auntie Em and Aunt Bossy grew pinker and pinker in the face as they strove to keep up with Mr Headmaster Hamm, who rowed in his shirt sleeves, singing the Volga Boat Song.

It was a hot summer's day. The lake lay like a sheet of glass, apart from the long ragged wake behind the boat. Since they all had their backs to the island they hit it long before they realized they had arrived, and the jolt crushed Aunt Millicent's legs between the strawberry tarts and the ginger-beer bottles.

The strawberry jam oozed on to her shins convincing her that she was bleeding to death. She lay back fainting in the arms of Mr Headmaster Hamm, until little John Henry remarked that Aunt Millicent's blood looked just like his favourite jam, whereupon she sat up in a minute, and told him that he was a very disgusting little boy.

Aunt Bossy decided that the boat should be tied

up in the shade of some willow trees and the provisions left inside it to keep cool until dinner-time. The boys were very disappointed, for they were all hungry and thought it must be long past dinner-time already.

'You boys can go and play,' Aunt Bossy told them. She gave them the cricket stumps, the bat and ball, and the rope to jump over, but they did not want to jump or play cricket. They wanted to rush about the island and explore, to look for birds' nests and to climb trees, to play at cowboys and Indians and to swim in the lake.

But all the aunts began to make aunt-noises at once:

'Don't get too hot!'

'Don't get too cold!'

'Don't get dirty!'

'Don't get wet!'

'Keep your hats on or you'll get sunstroke!'

'Keep your shoes on or you'll cut your feet!'

'Keep out of the water or you'll be drowned!'

'Don't fight!'

'Don't shout!'

'Be good!'

'Be good!'

'Be good!'

'There! You hear what your aunts say,' added Mr Headmaster Hamm. 'So mind you are good!'

The six aunts and Mr Headmaster Hamm went to sit under the trees to knit and embroider and play the fiddle, leaving the boys standing on the shore, looking gloomily at one another.

'Let's not,' said Adolphus.

'But if we aren't,' said Edward, 'we shan't get any dinner.'

'Let's have dinner first,' suggested little John Henry.

They sat down on the grass above the willow trees looking down on the boat. It was a long time since breakfast and they could not take their eyes off the boxes of provisions tucked underneath the seats, the bottles of ginger pop restored to order, and Auntie Em's basket of shining, rosy apples.

Voices came winging across the island:

'Why are you boys sitting there doing nothing at all? Why can't you find something nice to do on this lovely island?'

Quite coldly and firmly Freddie stood up and faced his brothers.

'Shall we leave them to it?' he suggested.

'What do you mean?' cried Adolphus, Edward, Montague, Montmorency and little John Henry.

'We'll take the boat and the provisions and row away to the other end of the lake, leaving them behind!' said Freddie calmly.

'Leave them behind on the island!' his brothers echoed faintly.

As the monstrous suggestion sank into their minds all six boys began to picture the fun they might have if they were free of the aunts and of Mr Headmaster Hamm. As if in a dream they followed Freddie to the boat, stepped inside and cast off the rope. At the very last moment Adolphus flung the

suitcase of sandwiches ashore before each boy
seized an oar and rowed for their lives away from
the island.

By the time the six aunts and Mr Headmaster
Hamm had realized what was happening the boat
was well out into the lake, and the boys took not
the slightest notice of the waving handkerchiefs,
the calls, the shouts, the pleadings and even the
bribes that followed them across the water.

It was a long, hard pull to the end of the lake

but not a boy flagged until the bows of the boat touched shore and the island was a blur in the far distance. Then, rubbing the blistered palms of their hands, they jumped ashore, tying the rope to a rock, and tossing the provisions from one to another in a willing chain.

Then began the most unforgettable afternoon of their lives. It started with a feast, when each boy stuffed himself with whatever he fancied most. Ginger-beer bottles popped and fizzed, apple cores were tossed far and wide. When they had finished eating they amused themselves by writing impolite little messages to their aunts and to Mr Headmaster Hamm, stuffing them into the empty bottles and sending them off in the direction of the little island.

They wrote such things as:

> 'Hey diddle diddle
> Old Ham and his fiddle
> Sharp at both ends
> And flat in the middle!'

'Aunt Miranda has got so thin
She has got nothing to keep her inside in.'

'My Aunt Boss rides a hoss.
Which is boss, hoss or Boss?'

Fortunately, since they forgot to replace the stoppers, all the bottles went to the bottom long before they reached their goal.

After this they swam in the lake, discovering enough mud and weeds to plaster themselves with dirt until they looked like savages. Drying themselves on the trousers of their sailor suits they dressed again and rushed up into the hills beyond the lake where they discovered a cave, and spent an enchanting afternoon playing at robbers, and hurling great stones down the steep hillside.

Feeling hungry again the boys ate the rest of the provisions, and then, too impatient to wait for the dark, decided to let off the box of fireworks. Even by daylight these provided a splendid exhibition as Freddie lit one after another. Then a spark fell on Montague's collar, burning a large hole, while Montmorency burnt his hand and hopped about crying loudly. To distract him Freddie lit the largest rocket of all, which they had been keeping for the last.

They all waited breathlessly for it to go off, watching the little red spark creep slowly up the twist of paper until it reached the vital spot. With a tremendous hiss the rocket shot into the air. Montmorency stopped sucking his hand and all the boys cheered.

But the rocket hesitated and faltered in mid-flight. It turned a couple of somersaults in the air and dived straight into the boat, landing in the bows with a crash.

Before it could burn the wood or do any damage Freddie rushed after it. With a prodigious bound he leapt into the boat that had drifted a few yards from the shore.

Unfortunately he landed so heavily that his foot

went right through one of the boards, and although he seized the stick of the rocket and hurled it far into the lake, the water came through the hole so quickly that the fire would have been quenched in any case.

There was nothing that any of them could do, for the boat was rotten, and the plank had simply given way. They were forced to stand and watch it sink before their eyes in four feet of water.

The sun was setting now. The surrounding hills threw blue shadows into the lake. A little breeze sprang up ruffling the water. The island seemed infinitely far away.

Soberly, sadly, the six boys began to walk down the shore to the beginning of the lake, not knowing what they would do when they got there. They were exhausted by their long, mad afternoon – some were crying and others limping.

Secretly the younger ones hoped that when they arrived they would find the grown-ups waiting for them, but when they reached the beginning of the lake no grown-ups were there. Not even Davy Driver.

'We will build a fire!' Freddie announced to revive their spirits. 'It will keep us warm and show the aunts we are all safe and well.'

'They get so anxious about us!' said Montmorency.

So they built an enormous bonfire from all the driftwood and dry branches they could find. This cheered them all very much because they were strictly forbidden to make bonfires at home.

It was dark by now, but they had the fire for light, and suddenly the moon rose, full and stately, flooding the lake with a sheet of silver. The boys laughed and shouted. They flung more branches on to the fire and leapt up and down.

Suddenly Adolphus stopped in mid-air and pointed, horror-struck, towards the water.

Far out on the silver lake, sharply outlined

against the moonlight, they saw a sight that froze their blood to the marrow.

It was the aunts' hats, drifting towards the shore.

The same little breeze that rippled the water and fanned their fire was blowing the six hats away from the island, and as they floated closer and closer to the shore the boys realized for the first time what a terrible thing they had done, for kind Aunt Bossy, generous Aunt Millicent, good Aunt Celestine, devoted Aunt Miranda, worthy Aunt Adelaide and dear *dear* Auntie Em, together with their much respected headmaster, Mr Hamm, had all been DROWNED!

Freddie, Adolphus, Edward, Montague, Montmorency and little John Henry burst into tears of such genuine repentance and grief that it would have done their aunts good to hear them. They sobbed so bitterly that after a while they had no more tears left to weep, and it was little John Henry who first wiped his eyes on his sleeve and recovered his composure. The next moment his mouth opened wide and his eyes seemed about to burst out of his head.

He pointed a trembling finger towards the lake and all his brothers looked where he was pointing. Then their eyes bulged too and their mouths dropped open as they beheld the most extraordinary sight they had ever dreamed of.

The aunts were swimming home!

For under the hats there were heads, and behind the heads small wakes of foam bore witness to the efforts of the swimmers.

The hats were perfectly distinguishable. First came Aunt Bossy's blue hydrangeas topped by a purple bow, then Aunt Millicent's little lilac bonnet. Close behind Aunt Millicent came Aunt Celestine's boater, smartly ribboned in green plush, followed by Aunt Miranda's black velvet toque, with a bunch of violets. Then some yards farther from the shore a floral platter of pansies and roses that Aunt Adelaide had bought to open a Church Bazaar. And last of all came Auntie Em in her pink straw pillbox hat, dragging behind her with a rope the picnic suitcase, on which was seated Mr Headmaster Hamm, who could not swim.

Holding the sides of the suitcase very firmly with both hands, he carried between his teeth, as a dog carries a most important bone, the aunts' cane.

Motionless and petrified, with terror and relief boiling together in their veins, Freddie, Adolphus, Edward, Montague, Montmorency and little John Henry stood on the shore – the fire shining on their filthy suits, dirty faces and sodden shoes, while

slowly, steadily, the aunts swam back from the island, and far behind them over the hills appeared at last the lights of Davy Driver's wagonette, coming to fetch them home.

THE CRUEL NAUGHTY BOY

There was a cruel naughty boy,
  Who sat upon the shore,
A-catching little fishes by
  The dozen and the score.

And as they squirmed and wriggled there,
  He shouted loud with glee,
'You surely cannot want to live,
  You're little-er than me.'

Just then with a malicious leer,
  And a capacious smile,
Before him from the water deep
  There rose a crocodile.

He eyed the little naughty boy,
    Then heaved a blubbering sigh,
And said, 'You cannot want to live,
    You're little-er than I.'

The fishes squirm and wriggle still,
    Beside that sandy shore,
The cruel little naughty boy,
    Was never heard of more.

Anon.

ANDREW'S BEDTIME STORY

I told him a tale that I adore
Called Theseus and the Minotaur,
Of how a prince with a ball of wool
  That his girl friend Ariadne gave him,
Was forced to search for a fiery bull
  Through cave and labyrinth. Keen to save him,
She said, 'Unwind the wool as you go
Through the twisting corridors down below,
And return to me safe – I love you so.'

That was the start of the tale I told,
And Andrew listened, as good as gold.
Next day when he ran home from school,
He found a skein of his mother's wool,
Unwound it, tied it to door and chair,

Along the passage and up the stair,
     Yes, everywhere.
I opened the door of my room
     To find
Pitschi the cat with his legs entwined,
Jane and Helen flat on the floor,
Great-aunt almost sliced at the knees
(As wire at the grocer's slices cheese),
     All of them trapped.
     The thread I snapped,
With scissors and knife I hacked away
     And set them free.
     But where was A?
There, in a corner lurking, laughing.
     'No more
Of Ariadne's thread,
My boy,' I cried, 'or we'll all be dead!'
     I stalked away.
But a murderous thread not seen before
Tripped me up, and I cracked my head.

Ian Serraillier

Grateful acknowledgements are due to the following:
Richard Armstrong for 'Timmo in the Forest'; Dorothy
Clewes for 'Finding's Keeping'; Eileen Colwell for 'The
Boy Who Made Faces'; Helen Cresswell for 'The
Wigglish Tooth'; Alex Hamilton for 'The Wind That
Wanted Its Own Way'; Charlotte Hough, Faber & Faber
and McCall Publishing Co., New York, for 'The
Tidying Up of Thomas', from *Sir Frog and Other Stories*;
Carolyn Haywood and William Morrow & Co. Inc. for
'Eddie and the Goat', from *Eddie and the Fire Engine*
(copyright © 1949); Janet McNeill for 'The Gigantic
Badness'; Lance Salway for 'The Boy Who Wasn't Bad
Enough'; Barbara Softly for 'Paul and the Hungry
Tomatoes'; H. E. Todd for 'Timothy Puddlc'; Ursula
Moray Williams for 'A Picnic with the Aunts'; Ian
Serraillier and Oxford University Press for 'Andrew's
Bedtime Story', from *Happily Ever After*; and Gelett
Burgess for 'Table Manners'

Some other Young Puffins

Burglar Bells

John Escott

Bernie and Lee embark on a spot of detective work after they see a man climbing through the window of an empty house. They enlist the help of Rosemary and together the three set out to trap the man who they are convinced is the villain. But it is a handbell that catches the real burglar!

Duck Boy

Christobel Mattingley

The holiday at Mrs Perry's farm doesn't start too well for Adam. His older brother and sister don't want to play with him because he's too young. At first he's bored and lonely, but then he discovers the creek and meets two old ducks who obviously need some help – every year their eggs are stolen by rats or foxes, so Adam strikes a bargain with them – he'll help guard their nest if they'll let him learn to swim in their creek.

Three Cheers for Ragdolly Anna

Jean Kenward

Being a very special kind of doll, Ragdolly Anna is trusted to do all sorts of things for the Little Dressmaker, but somehow nothing ever seems to go right. Her balcony garden turns into a jungle, a misguided stranger hands her into a lost property office, and she's nearly bought as a fairy for a Christmas tree!

Dinner at Alberta's
Russell Hoban

Arthur the crocodile has extremely bad table manners until he is invited to dinner at Alberta's house.

The Great Piratical Rumbustification
Margaret Mahy

The Terrapin boys' babysitter turns out to be a pirate, and what better place than the Terrapins' house for a very special pirate party?

I'm Trying To Tell You
Bernard Ashley

If you had a chance to talk about your school, what would you say ... honestly? Nerissa, Ray, Lyn and Prakash are all in the same class at Saffin Street School but each of them has something different to say and a different story to tell – all with a real sense of humour that will particularly appeal to readers of about eight.

Stories for Under-Fives
Stories for Five-Year-Olds
Stories for Six-Year-Olds
Stories for Seven-Year-Olds
More Stories for Seven-Year-Olds
Stories for Eight-Year-Olds
Stories for Nine-Year-Olds
Sara and Stephen Corrin

Celebrated anthologies of stories especially chosen for each age group and tested in the classroom by the editors.

The Worst Witch
The Worst Witch Strikes Again
A Bad Spell for the Worst Witch

Jill Murphy

Mildred Hubble is the most disastrous dunce of all at
Miss Cackle's training school for witches. But even the
worst witch scores the occasional triumph!

Albert
Albert on the Farm

Alison Jezard

Albert is a lively and lovable bear – whatever he and his
friends are up to always turns into an uproarious
adventure.

The Old Nurse's Stocking-Basket

Eleanor Farjeon

'Children,' said the old Nurse, 'stop quarrelling, or you
know what,' and the children always stopped quarrelling
at once, for none of them wanted to miss her captivating
bedtime tales about the little princes and princesses, sea-
captains and peasants' sons and daughters she had known
in hundreds and hundreds of years as a children's nurse.

Two Village Dinosaurs

Phyllis Arkle

Two dinosaurs spell double trouble as Dino and Sauro
trample their amiable way through the village, causing
chaos and confusion on every side!

The Dwarfs of Nosegay
Paul Biegel

There are at least a hundred of the tiny moorland dwarfs whose favourite food is honey squeezed from heather bells, but Peter Nosegay, the smallest and youngest, is the bravest and cleverest of them all, and the kindest too.

Once Upon a Rhyme
Sara and Stephen Corrin

From skyscrapers to Guy Fawkes, ducks on a pond to rosebuds, and pirates to man-eating alligators: Sara and Stephen Corrin, so well known for their collections of stories for children, have put the spontaneous relish back into young children's poetry reading with this delicious selection of poems young children will really enjoy.

A Walk Down the Pier
John Escott

When part of the pier drops in the sea, Davy is in a dilemma – how can he get help for Mr Pennyquick, who lies injured in the pavilion at the end of the pier?

The Ghost Elephant
Alan C. Jenkins

The story of an African village in which the inhabitants believe they are being haunted by the ghost of an elephant they had hunted. (*Original*)

Victor the Vulture
Jane Holiday

Everyone in his class had a pet except Garth, so when his father won a vulture in a raffle it seemed like the answer to his prayers. But the local council have rules about their tenants keeping pets . . .